ROSEMARY

Books by Mary Stolz

Rosemary

BY MARY STOLZ

HARPER & ROW, PUBLISHERS

New York, Evanston, and London

To Edward

ROSEMARY

CHAPTER ONE

IN A SENSE, JAY ETTING HAD PICKED HER UP. IT HADN'T seemed so to Rosemary at the time. It had seemed romantic. It became clear what Jay thought, though, rather quickly.

He had come into the department store with Helena Williams, a girl Rosemary had known in high school and who had gone on to the college in town. Jay was slim, with handsome features and good, indifferently worn clothes. He looked like a college student painted for an advertisement, and therefore Rosemary found him wonderful. She liked the sound of his voice, and his tilted grin. She liked him so much, so quickly, that she pushed aside her pride and called, "Hi, Helena, how are you?" For a hot, frightening moment, she thought Helena was not going to reply at all, and by the time the reply came a faint flush marked Rosemary's cheeks.

"Oh, yes," Helena said. "Rosemary. So here's where you work." Her voice was only just not insolent, and she made it clear she would not be detained for purposes of chatting. She almost tugged at Jay, saying, "If we're going to get the stuff and get back in time to decorate, we'll have to hurry."

But Jay said, "Hold on," and glanced at Rosemary with a smile that seemed to affect only one half of his mouth. "You should have some suggestions," he said to her. "Since you work here, and all. We want to get stuff to festoon the gymnasium for the shindig this Saturday." He spoke as if Rosemary, naturally, would know to what shindig he referred. "Your friend Helena here can't even go to it, and she's helping to decorate anyway. Tell me, was she always this unselfish?"

"We didn't know each other very well," Helena said, and then with an effort, "Rosemary, this is Jay Etting. Rosemary—Reed, Jay. She and I were in high school together, that's all."

"But what can be nicer than an old school friendship?" he drawled.

Rosemary said quickly, "As Helena says, we didn't know each other very well," and realized with regret that it was a fairly conclusive sentence. "About the decorations . . . I mean, what sort did you have in mind? I could tell you where to go—"

Could you, indeed? said Helena's eyes. But she smiled and murmured how kind, and a fall motif was what they had in mind. That is, her voice implied, if you know what a motif is.

Rosemary lifted her chin a little. "Why don't you try a vegetable store? Real fruits and vegetables are much nicer, I think, than those imitation ones."

"It's a good idea," Helena admitted. "And then the

2

stuff could be put in those baskets we send around for Thanksgiving, couldn't it, Jay?" She turned to him eagerly. "Oh, come *on*. We really do have to rush." She started off, forcing him to follow, turned and threw a casual, "Nice to have seen you," to Rosemary. Jay gave her a little flick of the fingers and that smile again, and they were gone. Rosemary stared at the door through which they'd disappeared until the section manager came across and suggested if she was that anxious to get outdoors . . . he left the implication unsaid, and Rosemary hurried to escape it.

She thought about him all day, and that night before she fell asleep, made up a little scene in which he'd come to her and say, "I couldn't stay away, you see. I've thought about you and thought about you until I simply had to see you." She composed it one way and then another, first having them meet accidentally in the street, then having him call at her home (he would have gone immediately to the phone book after leaving Helena), then at the store. *I've thought about you and thought about you.*

It was a long time before she got to sleep.

And the very next day, as she turned to hand a customer a package, her startled eyes encountered his smiling ones. Still holding the package, unable to speak, Rosemary looked at him and felt a giddy, mounting happiness. Was it possible to dream a thing so intensely that it had to come true? Was it—

"Miss, if you don't mind, I'd like to have my stockings." The customer sounded only mildly annoyed, and

3

she regarded the two young people with interest. Jay returned her glance with easy friendliness.

Rosemary turned her head dreamily, looked at her hands, still clutching the woman's purchase. "I'm sorry, ma'am." She thrust the package across the counter.

"Quite all right," said the woman, her attention now entirely on Jay. She gave him a final leisurely glance and walked away, smiling faintly.

"Good-looking gal," Jay said, looking after her, and then turned to Rosemary. "Surprised to see me?"

"Yes, I am," she said softly.

"Thought you'd be."

He grinned, and Rosemary's hands trembled a little. He's wonderful, she thought, knowing nothing about him, reading into him anything she wished. He's wonderful, and he wanted to see me again.

"I had an idea yesterday," he said. "Couldn't, of course, mention it then. Under the circumstances."

"No. I mean yes. I see that you couldn't."

"Want to know what it was?" he asked. He seemed to enjoy dallying, drawing the matter out. Not like Reg, who rushed at any point as if it were an objective to be taken. "No sense beating around the bush," he'd say, and crash right through it. She had a moment's pang at her disloyalty, then looked at Jay and forgot Reg altogether.

She relaxed, and smiled a little, and said, "I guess I'd like to know. Something nice?"

"Depends." He leaned on the counter. "*I* think it is."

"Oh, golly," Rosemary said under her breath, "here comes the section manager."

Jay said indolently, lifting his voice only a fraction, "Well, I don't exactly know her size. She's about so high—" he held his hand at shoulder height and straightened as though for that purpose "—and weighs in at a hundred and eighty."

Rosemary giggled as the frowning section manager hesitated, walked slowly on, his backward glance dubious.

"Think you can fix me up with something like that?" Jay asked solemnly. "Something tasty." He indicated a pair of sheer black stockings with rhinestone clocks.

"Do you really want those?"

"I certainly do not. Wrap up a pair in size nine and sourpuss over there can get on with his tour of duty." He thought a moment. "At that, I can send them to my sister for her birthday. That'd get a rise out of her."

Head down, Rosemary put the flimsy, glittery things in tissue, rang up the sale and handed him the package. His fingers caressed hers lightly as he took it, and a tingle of pleasure darted through her whole being. He knows it, too, she thought, glancing up to meet his eyes. I've seen him twice, talked to him for five minutes, and I'm lost, and he knows precisely what he's done. She made a nervous gesture, almost as if she reached for her pride, and then sighed a little as it eluded her.

"Why so pensive, fair one?" he asked with amusement.

"Just . . . thinking," she said helplessly.

"It becomes you." He fingered his package and added, "Before any more petty overlords or customers get in our way, I'll tell you what my thought was. In a word, since Helena, who's a sort of section manager in *her* way, won't be in these parts on Saturday, I wondered if you'd take her place for me."

Rosemary caught her breath. Take Helena's place? Go to a dance—a shindig—at the college? Would you like to visit heaven this coming Saturday, Rosemary? Would you like to—

"Oh, I'd love it," she breathed. "I'd . . . I mean, that would be very nice."

Jay grinned. "I liked it better the first time. However, that's settled, and I'm enraptured, and if you'll scribble the address on this sales slip, please, I'll be around to get you when the clock strikes eight."

Then he was gone, and this was only Wednesday.

Rosemary, on her lunch hour, went to the Junior Deb department, evening fashions, and moved dreamily from rack to rack, studying price tags, computing her pay envelope, her expenses, the store's discount, returning to the price tags.

"Something—" said a saleswoman, patting her hair and starting across the floor, and then, "Oh, it's you, dearie. Going to shoot the works?"

"Such as they are," Rosemary said, adding in a burst of uncontrollable delight, "I've been invited to a thing —a shindig—a dance—at the college."

"Going to wear the same dress to all three?"

They smiled at each other, made warm and friendly, though they were scarcely acquainted, through Rosemary's pleasure and their mutual lack of money. "Got a real nice little number over here," the saleswoman said, "and not too much, considering."

"I can't pay more than—I honestly shouldn't spend more than twenty."

The saleswoman slowed. "Well, I dunno. Twenty. That one'd be thirty with the discount, so there's no point looking at it. Let's see, now . . ."

"I want to look at it," Rosemary said, because she had already seen the dummy toward which they were walking. A flame-colored gown, tight to the hips, with a rounded neckline, small cap sleeves, and a great full skirt. She'd wear it with the gold slippers she already owned, and her hair in a pony tail with the gold clasp. It had to be this dress, of course, at thirty dollars, though she could not actually afford even the twenty. I'll give it to myself for Christmas, for my birthday, for anything at all, she told herself. A present, for getting to go to college after all.

"Nylon acetate," the saleswoman explained, taking a size twelve from the rack. "Looks just like a slubbed silk, doesn't it?"

The dress was hers, as if the designer had had no one else in mind. I'll be just as pretty as they are, she told herself, turning before the long mirror. Prettier than some, and as well dressed as any. She smiled, as though she'd entered a battle and emerged victorious, though the enemy was a shadow—the *they* of her mind—and no battle had been engaged or even decided.

"I'll take it," she sighed, and reluctantly drew the dress over her head and gave it to be wrapped. It was only Wednesday and she did not see how Saturday could ever come.

Thursday. Then Friday. Somehow they contrived to present themselves, inch past, and be gone. Saturday. She worked all day, charming, almost mesmerizing customers and section manager alike with her airy spirits. Tonight, tonight, she chanted to herself. How in the world could one person *contain* so much happiness? If people get much happier than this, she thought, they must just simply float away and never come back to earth again, never work nor eat nor wonder what's to pay. Over and over, her mouth quivered into smiles and her eyes closed and she saw herself floating—flying— over a dance floor in her flame-colored dress among the college people. They would whisper and say, "Who is she? Who is that lovely girl, and where has she been till now?" Now everything began. She and Lenore would get to know people at the college. Girls—it was possible—would stop by of an evening for a Coke and gossip. And boys—well, Jay was enough. The thought of Helena flickered briefly through her mind, but could not stay. I'll take my chances and Helena will have to take hers, Rosemary thought. She was filled with self-confidence. Because, after all, unless he were very much attracted, a boy wouldn't stop by again that way, after only a few words of conversation, and ask for a date. It was probably very unusual to have such a thing happen to—

"I dislike to break into your reverie, Miss Reed, but these two customers—"

Still, the section manager spoke mildly, and the two women smiled. Everyone loved her today. It was an omen, she decided. *I am a vessel of happiness.* That was the sort of thing Rosemary liked to say that made Reg mutter uncomfortably. Not that she'd ever said that to him, but any extravagance in speech received no welcome from Reg.

"Can't you say what you mean?" he'd ask with a pained expression. "A tree's a tree. Do you have to call it an archangel on a hill?"

"But look at it, Reg. See how the branches sweep back like wings? And after all, you must admit it *is* on a hill. Don't you think it's beautiful?" she'd insist, when he didn't answer.

"Sure, it's a pretty *tree*," he'd say pointedly.

And at that, Rosemary had to admit that at times she felt a little foolish herself at the phrases that came into her mind. Overdramatic, and sometimes insincere. Nevertheless, today she *was* a vessel of happiness.

Lenore said she'd get the dinner and do the dishes. "You have to save yourself for the ball," she said sternly.

Rosemary was pressing the shimmering folds of her dress. "The whole thing feels sort of like Cinderella, doesn't it?" She looked around the kitchen. "Throw a few ashes in the corner there, will you, Lenore?" she said to her younger sister. "I'll sit in them for a bit before my bath."

"Well, darling, you're a step up on Cinderella as far

as I'm concerned. You did it all yourself. No assistance from fairy godmothers."

Rosemary's eyes glowed softly. "Do you think I'll get scared, Lennie? I mean, I'm not yet, but I bet I come all over cold and trembly." Thinking about it gave her the faintest touch of actual chill, but she grinned and pretended she'd been joking. Why had she had to think of it at all? Scared, indeed. She took a deep breath, held the dress up and then touched it to Lenore's cheek. "It is like silk, isn't it?"

"It's beautiful."

"Did Pop . . . did he say anything to you? About the money, I mean?"

"Just how much was it? I told him what you said to say."

They looked at each other uneasily. "It doesn't *look* shopworn enough so you'd get it for ten dollars," Lenore said.

"Pop won't know. And it'd make him nervous that I spent thirty." Rosemary thought a moment and added, "Makes me nervous."

"You needed it, and it's beautiful on you, and I'm glad you got it."

Rosemary agreed, but still the feeling could not be completely ignored—the sense of having spent, for her own pleasure, money that they all worked for and needed. It put a shadow on the sparkling happiness she'd felt all day. Some people, she thought, can make extravagant gestures and then say, Well, it's done, so it's done, don't let it spoil its own purpose. But Rosemary, who could not help making such gestures, could not, either, quite adjust to them. She stood now, the cooling iron heavy in her hands, and stared at the linoleum.

"Rosemary." Lenore's voice was peremptory. "You forget about it this minute. Anyway, I can wear the dress, can't I, sometimes?"

"Of course you can."

"Then it's an investment. Sooner or later we'd have needed one, and now we've got it." Lenore took the iron, stored it away, reached up for the dress that was suspended on a hanger from the top of the kitchen door, and firmly led the way upstairs. "I'll run your bath while you cream your face, and would you like a little soft music to get you back in the mood?"

Rosemary, following her sister into their room, laughed. "Your voice is all the music anyone could want, Lennie. And I'm already back in the mood."

The dress lay across the bed, and the water ran bubbling into the tub, and outside a true pumpkin-colored harvest moon moved tranquilly up the sky. Rosemary wrapped her hair in a towel and sat at the dressing table. She was singing as she rubbed the cold cream over her face.

Lenore and Hank left before Jay arrived. Lenore was disappointed, and Hank determined.

"I wouldn't miss the start of the game if the Shah of Iran was coming here," he told Lenore.

"But you've seen a thousand basketball games, and

I've never seen Jay Etting," she said, not really protesting. This, after all, was Hank. In Lenore's mind, when you'd said that, you'd said all that mattered.

"I intend," Hank said, "to see a thousand more, and all from start to finish." He leaned over and kissed her brow. "That is, unless you'd really rather wait and meet the guy."

Rosemary, in the brilliant gown, heard them as she descended the stairs, and felt the familiar brief catch at her heart. They were so . . . so much in love, so *kind* to each other. She thought, suddenly, that she'd never realized how much a part of love was kindness. Of, in any case, the sort of love Hank and Lenore had. And that seemed to her the best love possible. There were kids who went together in high school and you somehow knew it to be a high school thing, a stopgap, a way of passing time, no matter how ardent they seemed. But Hank and Lenore—she could no more imagine their parting than—than, she concluded for herself, I can imagine myself and a boy in love that way. She shook her head impatiently. *Why* did she have to think of things like that, think of things which cut across her joy like trailing shadows?

"Oh, now, gosh, they'll have to picket you," Hank said, looking at Rosemary and awarding her a low whistle. "Unfair to organized college girls." His voice was unreservedly admiring.

"Like it?" Rosemary asked with pleasure.

Hank continued to study her gleaming hair and dress, her shining deep brown eyes. "Well," he said at length, "it's too bad for you, Lenore, but I've just given my heart to Rosemary."

"I warn you, I'll fight," Lenore said.

"Won't do you a bit of good. When I give a thing, I give it."

"But I haven't given it back to you yet," Lenore smiled, and his glance moved back to hers with infinite tenderness. "No, but really," Lenore said quickly, "doesn't she look marvelous?"

"She does. You're a marvelous pair of sisters." He took Rosemary by the shoulders and turned her slowly around. "Yup, just as I thought, beautiful all the way around." He looked at his watch. "Say, Rosemary, you wouldn't mind if we left now, would you? That game—"

"For goodness' sakes, of course I don't mind. Go along and have a wonderful time and drive carefully."

Lenore, as she was leaving, turned impulsively and kissed her sister. "You have fun, Rosie," she said. "Lots of fun."

When they were gone, Rosemary walked about idly, glanced two or three times in the hall mirror, clasped her hands together to subdue a slight tremor, finally sat on the edge of an overstuffed chair, shoulders back, skirt spread carefully about her.

She waited.

Outside, on their heavily traveled street, traffic was a continuous low clamor. Horns, tires, brakes, occasional yelled insults were an accompaniment to their lives that she scarcely noticed until such a time as this, when she sat in the empty house, waiting in emptiness for the doorbell to sound. Within, there were the usual house sounds . . . shifting of boards, faint complaint of the furnace, ticking of the big alarm clock in the kitchen. Once she thought she heard a mouse in the walls. These were sounds, also, that she usually ignored without knowing she did, and now could not ignore though she tried. She held her hands together and looked around the room and breathed deeply. Then she jumped to her feet and went into the kitchen. Eight-twenty. She ran the faucet till the water was cold, drank a little, wandered back to the living room again. What she was beginning to believe, she would not admit. And yet it did happen to people. What in the world would she do? What did people do who had spent too much money on a dress, and put it on with care and long preparation and a heart bounding with nervous happiness after days and slow days of waiting, only to have the minutes and then the hours go by with no step on the porch, no ring at the door?

The doorbell rang, and she had not heard the step on the porch. For a moment, relief weakened her so that she could not move, and then, with a resurgence of all the bliss she'd felt that morning, she ran to let Jay Etting in, flinging the door back, and laughing up at him. She stood so for a moment, the laughter and pleasure caught on her face like a photograph, then slowly draining, slowly changing to bewilderment, uncertainty, and finally to fear. What had she done wrong? What was *wrong*?

"What is it?" she cried desperately. "Is there . . . what's wrong?"

Jay Etting licked his lips uneasily, then walked in past her, closing the door. "My fault, I suppose," he said. He sounded both chagrined and annoyed. "My fault, but I didn't know you'd—"

"I'd what?" she demanded when he hesitated.

"Well, that you'd . . . take it for granted we were going to the Thanksgiving Dance. Oh, now don't look that way. I said it was my—"

"I don't know what you mean," she faltered. "I don't understand. Didn't you invite me to it? Didn't you say that since Helena—" She could not go on. Turning, she started for the stairs, veered and headed for the living room, spun around again to face him. "What *did* you mean?"

"Well, I sort of thought—you know—a movie or something, and then dancing at a tavern—"

"A tavern. I see." She lifted her head, vowing to herself that she would not cry. I promise you, Rosemary, she said in silent anguish, that you are not going to cry. "We misunderstood each other," she managed at length. "Now, if you'll please go—"

"Hey now, don't get in a huff—"

Huff, she repeated to herself. All the days of waiting. Our thirty dollars. The . . . happiness. And he tells me not to get in a huff. Vaguely she thought that the time could come when this would not seem important. The time could come. Good enough for movies and taverns, but never, not by any means, good enough to get to that college. She thought suddenly of Lenore, and her eyes closed briefly. Thank heaven Lenore had not waited, had not been here for this. Then she was laughing. "You know," she gulped, "it really does strike me as rather silly. I mean, after all, a bit more money and I *could* be in that college. A scholarship, a different attitude in Pop, oh, any number of ways I could have been there. And just because I'm not, then I'm not good enough for a dance even. Why there are girls at that college I wouldn't have in the house—" She didn't know whether this was true, but said it in her wildly laughing voice. "Boys, too, I might add. Boys, too—"

"Stop that, for Pete's sake," he shouted. "You're hysterical, or something."

That sobered her. She grasped the newel post for support, and nodded weakly. Yes, she was a bit hysterical, and that was possibly worse than crying. "I'm sorry," she said with an effort. "And I wish you'd go."

"If you'd listen to me for a moment—" He hesitated, and Rosemary, contemptuous of herself, waited. "It's like this," he went on. "Helena—that is, she and I—" He did not trouble to finish that. "She'd be madder than hops if she found out I took another girl to the dance. I mean, that girl's got a terrible temper, and she's so darned possessive it's alarming," he finished complacently. "But, you see—"

"And if she found out you'd taken another girl to a tavern?" Rosemary interrupted stiffly.

"Well—but I didn't think she'd find out."

I'm tired, Rosemary thought. She ran a hand through her hair and looked up at him. "All right, you've explained. I really do wish you'd leave."

"No," he said abruptly. "Get your wrap. We'll go to the dance."

She felt no triumph at all. She felt, precisely, nothing. "Thank you, but no."

"Oh, don't be sulky, Rosemary," Jay said, moving nearer to her. "Come on with me."

Perhaps it was that his voice had gotten softer, or that he'd used her name. Perhaps it was because of Lenore, hoping so much for the evening. Perhaps it was for the flame-colored gown. Maybe for reasons she couldn't even recognize, but after a moment's hesitation, Rosemary got her coat from the closet, held it for him to take, and slid her arms into the sleeves. As he relinquished the coat, Jay put his hands on her shoulders, and instantly the shock of delight ran through her. He tightened his grip a little and then released her. And he knows, she thought. Just as he knew in the store the other day. She thought that was probably why he'd decided to run the risk of Helena's anger. (I remember Helena, she thought, as reserved and terribly proud. I never remember her being angry so that it would show.) Any boy likes to feel he can, with the mere touch of his hands, quicken a girl's pulse beyond her ability to conceal. (Was that what he had done with Helena? Broken her defenses?)

And yet, riding beside him in the darkened car, eying sideways his blunt good-looking profile, she was glad once again, as she'd been—almost as she'd been—in the morning. Why shouldn't she be able to . . . She did not quite put into words the thought that lay behind them, but a vision of sometime in the future, when she and Jay would be walking together, on a spring day, maybe, across the campus, teased at her and would not pronounce itself impossible. She could hear his voice saying, "What if I'd gone that night? What if you'd been so angry . . . Oh, Rosemary, what a fool I was!" And her own voice answering, "But I didn't get so angry . . . and you aren't a fool, Jay—Jay, darling." "Darling. Say that again, Rosemary . . . ."

"Watcha thinking about?" he asked, and he leaned over to push the lighter in, his hand trailing lightly over her knee.

He likes to touch me, Rosemary thought. It frightened her, filled her with peculiar bliss, and the knowledge that she wanted him to weakened her muscles. I've been in love before, she thought . . . she had to admit that she had been in love over and over. But never like this. Never had she felt the way she felt now about Jay.

He stopped for a red light, lit his cigarette, glanced at her with a slow smile. In the half-light from the street, he seemed to Rosemary the most wonderful-looking creature she'd ever seen. "Too bad it's too late to get you a corsage," he said, his voice low.

"It doesn't matter," she said fervently. "I really don't care at all."

Again he smiled, and then put the car in gear and continued toward the college.

The gymnasium was, indeed, festooned. It fairly sagged beneath the fall motif. Rosemary, entering the huge room, entering into the blare of a ten-piece orchestra riding over hundreds of dancing feet and voices that murmured and laughed and called out to other voices, was stricken with fright. It was too big, this room, the dancers and the voices too sure of themselves. It was no place for Rosemary Reed, even if she'd dreamed of it for years. I don't belong here, she thought desperately. Whatever made me think that it would be all right, that my dress would be beautiful, that—

"Little girls' locker room over that way," Jay said, gesturing with his head. "You go fancy up and leave your coat, and I'll meet you here."

"You'll be sure to be here?" she said anxiously.

Jay lifted a humorous brow. "Well, natch," he drawled, and she flushed a little, turning away.

In the locker room she surrendered her coat in exchange for a ticket, then made her way to the mirrors. Looking at her dress, at the dresses of the girls around her, she relaxed a little. It really was pretty, just as pretty as any, and nicer than some. That, at least, was all right. These girls all talked to each other excitedly, exchanging combs and lipsticks, crowding and laughing. They neither talked to Rosemary nor ignored her. She didn't mind that, but began to wonder what she and Jay would do. Would they sit with other people? Or would they have to sit alone? And if they did, would that annoy him? Slowly she stored her lipstick and powder puff away, slowly went toward the door leading to the gym. Oh, Lenore, she mourned, if you could see me now. And she knew that Lenore, watching the basketball game in the high school gym, would be thinking of her sister, brilliantly happy and successful in the college gym. The thought of Lenore warmed her, and she went to Jay with a lightened step.

"I've managed to get us squeezed in with a bunch of clowns over there under the balcony," Jay said, taking her hand. "Let's toddle on over and secure our places before we dance, eh?"

"All right, Jay. I . . . will it be all right?"

"Will what be all right?"

"Me. I mean, having me?"

"What are you talking about? If I ask you, it's all right," he said, his voice slightly grouchy. Then he laughed. "Oh, you mean Helena. Well, like I said, or maybe I didn't, but anyway, she's got to learn she hasn't got a lien on me. Altogether too cocky, that lass. I'll— I mean, we'll show her."

Rosemary, recalling his touch, thought, That's not the only reason you're with me, Jay. She felt a little cocky herself.

The table was a long one, decorated with colored ears of corn, gourds, pumpkins, sheaves of wheat, already cluttered with overflowing ashtrays, glasses of soft drinks and beer, girls' handbags, pretzels, popcorn. Some of the chairs were pushed back, as departing dancers had left them. Those who remained waved desultorily or gaily to Jay, then returned to low, private conversations. A boy and a girl at the end never looked up. Their hands were locked, their faces close together, and they murmured to each other ceaselessly. Jay introduced Rosemary to the two nearest couples, saying their names so fast she couldn't follow, but they all looked at her keenly, studied Jay, and then became elaborately unmindful of the fact that Rosemary was not Helena.

They talked of things she didn't know about or understand. Passwords, she decided, looking from one speaker to another. She smiled when they glanced her way, but at what she couldn't tell. Certainly not at them. Their smiles for her were not real, and so hers for them could not be.

" . . . whatever became of the Hollowell business?" a red-haired girl was asking Jay.

"Yeah, how about that, boy?" said a big footballish-looking person down the table. "Give."

Jay shrugged.

"Now, come on, come on," they said imperiously.

"What was the Hollowell business?" Rosemary asked, and had the impression they all looked at her with surprise.

"Oh well," Jay said. He spread his hands. "Seems this fellow, name of Hollowell, wrote a song for the musical comedy we did last spring. And I wrote one, too. By some odd chance they sounded stunningly alike. He claimed I stole it, that's all."

"But what happened?"

"There was a mild skirmish in the backdrops, and he threatened to go to the Dean, but then I pointed out that he wasn't the only person who admired Bizet, and a slight study of the score would show where we'd both mined our diamonds. Or should I call them our rhinestones?" he added carelessly. "Bizet wasn't above a spot of plundering on that particular air himself."

Rosemary stared at him, speechless and shaken with admiration. He could write music! Oh, Jay, the admirable, Jay, the urbane, Jay, the everything a man should be. And he's with me, she told herself. I'm his date. Her heart swelled with pride and the unmatched, undreamed-of delight.

"But did you?" she asked breathlessly. "Take it from . . . Hollowell, I mean?"

"I heard him tinkling something catchy, *and* familiar, on the piano one day. You could make a case out of that, I suppose."

Rosemary only thought he was wonderful. "Whose did they use? I mean," she said, with a sensation of daring, "did they use your rhinestones or his?"

"Oh, mine, of course. I steal better than poor Hollowell did."

They all laughed, and some exchanged dry glances.

"Yeah, but how about that threat he made?" the football one asked. "Didn't he swear to get even with you after he'd graduated? That's what you said, anyway." *Was* there a hint of derision in his tone? Rosemary did not believe it.

"Oh, he threatened all right," Jay assured them. "And the upshot was that I met him in New York last summer and the clonk took me to lunch. We had a good laugh over the whole thing. Pals, we were, talking about the good old days, like they'd been peach brandy and ice cream and nothing but. Friends of the bosom, like Athos and his sidekick. Though just for that one lunch, mind you."

"I got to New York myself last summer," a boy interrupted. "Stopped in at—"

He went on, but Rosemary lost interest. She wished Jay would ask her to dance. Or, failing that for a little while, that he'd talk to her. Or that someone would. So far no one had addressed a direct remark to her, nor looked at her more than glancingly. So far—she lifted her glance and met the interested gaze of the football boy.

"Say," he said to Jay, "if you don't want to dance with coffee-eyes here, how about letting someone else?"

Rosemary felt a start of pleasure, and Jay turned to the speaker. "Take it easy, Rover, you'll have your chance." He pulled Rosemary to her feet, and, putting his arms about her, steered her expertly out on the waxed and gleaming floor.

She had known he would dance like this. He was an expression of the music, and it was almost like dancing with the music itself, turning and weaving in its very arms. She closed her eyes and leaned against him, and the pressure of his hand on her back grew warmer and harder. If they could only remain so, dancing till it was time to leave, never going back to that table where people seemed to feel she did not exist at all. She recalled without amusement, with embarrassment, her notion that this evening was going to mark the start of a new experience for her and Lenore. *Dates and girlish gossip.* It made her quiver a little.

Drawing her even closer, Jay said, "Well, the fat's in the fire, but darned if it isn't worth it."

With a sense of shock, Rosemary pulled away and stared up at him. "What do you mean?"

"Heck, you don't suppose that gang's going to keep Helena in the dark, do you?"

I didn't suppose you were thinking about her at all. "I didn't suppose anything," she said flatly. "Nothing at all." And though they continued to dance, it was all different. The music was only music, and Jay a good dancer. (Reg was a good dancer, too.) A good dancer who held her too close, though she strained away from him.

"C'mon now," he whispered. "Don't be mad. I shouldn't have mentioned her, darned fool that I was." He blew softly in her ear. "Rosemary, smile at me."

She looked up at him, and smiled, and looked away.

Presently the football boy cut in, and then others, and Rosemary showed every sign of being a belle. She was aware of talking a little too much, a little too loudly. Aware, too, that many of these boys were holding her closer than they should, but she laughed with them excitedly, and thought how Jay would certainly have to be proud of his date, his vivacious, popular, sought-after date. Was Helena ever this much in demand? She danced endlessly, and though the girls at the table ignored her more pointedly than they had earlier, Rosemary assured herself she didn't care. Piqued, probably. Or just plain unfriendly. She didn't care. She was at a college dance, and the boys liked her, and she was having fun.

When the band played "Good Night, Ladies," the girls began to gather their bags and head for the locker room, and Rosemary, crimson with shame, saw that they had no intention of waiting for her. She walked away, not looking back, pretending to be interested in nothing but the purely factual business of securing her coat, and she was back with Jay before any of the others appeared.

"Nice," he said. "Good dancer and prompt. What more could I ask of a girl?"

One of the boys laughed, but Jay ignored him. He held Rosemary's coat for her and said, "Let's go, shall we?"

"But—"

She broke off, drew a deep breath, and nodded. She had heard (how could she not have heard?) an earlier discussion about going out for scrambled eggs and coffee at a nearby diner. She and Jay, it seemed, were not included. All right, they weren't. She almost gritted her teeth as they went from the gymnasium into the cool, leaf-smoky night. It's nearly over, she said to herself. It's nearly over. I'll be home soon, and safe from them all, and I'll never, never . . . She got in the car wordlessly, and sank back, her eyes closed, waiting to be home.

Jay didn't drive far, and when he parked it was not in front of her house. It was on a road leading away from the campus, and here and there, in the dark, she could see other cars parked. So that was it. That, no doubt, was why the boy had laughed and why she and Jay had not been invited for scrambled eggs. Probably they thought she was just the type for this, and they hadn't wanted to delay his pleasure. She turned to him abruptly and was in his arms before a word could be spoken. Perhaps if he had spoken, or given her a chance to, it would not have been like this, she would not have pressed against him with this strange stinging sweetness, this sense of warm and human closeness after an evening of chill and exclusion. His lips were soft, and his hands warm, and she almost yielded, without thought, this thing that he seemed to want so passionately. And then, as if she'd been drowning and suddenly realized the need to struggle if she were to be saved, she wrenched away from him wildly, and neither his entreaties nor his strength nor his swift surliness could lure her back.

She huddled against the car door and said, "Take me home. I want you to take me home."

Jay studied her, then, a long moment. His expression was one of profound annoyance and when he spoke there was contempt distinct in his voice. "You know," he said, starting the car, "you've been practically begging for it all evening." Rosemary gasped, but he went on. "Not only from me. You crawled all over every guy you danced with. But—" he flicked a hand in the air "—so you changed your mind. Okay. Woman's privilege, I guess."

After that he drove in silence, not looking at Rosemary, who hunched in her corner staring at the road. When they arrived at her house, he got out of the car, went around to open the door for her, walked to the foot of the porch, and said quite easily, "Well, thanks. You're a good dancer, anyway."

Rosemary looked up at him without comprehension, then turned and went into the house.

Lenore was sitting up in bed, and she gave a squeal of greeting when Rosemary entered their room. "Hi, honey, I waited, you see, to—" She broke off, tipping her head, and jumped up, grabbing Rosemary's arm. "What's the matter, Rosie?" she asked tensely. "What is it? *Rosemary*, what's happened?"

Rosemary took a deep, convulsive breath and said in a stunned voice the only thing she could think of to say. "He made a pass at me."

Lenore's hand fell away. "Oh, but . . . but, golly, that happens. You don't have to act like your last hope of heaven had disappeared. You've certainly had fellows make passes at you before. You even," she said, attempting to smile, "liked it, sometimes, didn't you?"

"This was . . . he was . . . awful." What he *said* was awful. What he said was cruel and debasing and she was sick to the center of her heart at what he'd said. She would not tell that to Lenore.

Her sister suddenly moved around to face her directly. "Rosemary, you didn't . . . I mean, nothing *happened*, did it?"

"Oh, no, no . . . I wasn't . . . that isn't it . . . ."

She dropped to her bed and sat twisting her hands, the dress rumpling around her, her head falling forward till the brown hair tumbled. "No, no, Lenore. Don't worry. It's just that I . . . just that—" She could not go on.

Gently Lenore sat beside her and took her hand. "Well, he must have been pretty foul, to make you feel like this. And it's a shame," she said wistfully, "when we'd planned on it so, and all. But I should think you'd have more pride than to let it get you like this. Write him off, that's all. Forget about him."

You've been practically begging for it all evening. I'll never forget him. I'll remember him all my life. She turned to Lenore, blinking, and rubbed the corners of her eyes. "Sure, Lennie. That's the only thing to do. I guess I just—just sort of got thrown for a bit. I'll be all right." She stood up and removed the flame-colored gown. "You can have this."

"Oh, now—"

"Please. I'll never wear it again. But it'd look wonderful on you, and you can wear it to the Christmas formal."

Lenore tried not to look at the dress, failed, and could not help smiling. "It would be a nice change from the taffeta," she said, and into her eyes came the same dreamy look of future conquests, hinging on a dress, that had been in Rosemary's only a few hours before. "Funny, isn't it," she said, "how girls persist in believing a dress can change the world?"

Rosemary, going to the bathroom to wash, thought, Lenore knows where her conquests lie, and that makes all the difference. She leaned over and ran the bathtub water hard, because she wanted to cry, and then turned it off because she remembered that the sound of it would wake Pop. And their boarder, the gym teacher, would be sure to wake up and give them a lecture in the morning on the absolute necessity of undisturbed sleep. So she did not cry then.

The weeks passed, and she was never alone. She was always at the store, or there was someone in the house, or she was with Reg. When the time came when she finally was alone, it was too late to cry. She merely had to live with a harsh hurt that grew blunted with time but never, as she had known it would not, flowed entirely away to leave her in peace.

CHAPTER TWO

HELENA WILLIAMS CLOSED HER NOTEBOOK, ASSEMBLED
the reference books and textbooks she'd piled about the
library table, and got out her compact, turning her head
this way and that. She decided she didn't need lipstick,
and got up, brushing her skirt down. It was rather late.
Too late now to wash her hair before going to bed, and
she'd wanted to do that. But at least the paper was
started. She was not going to be caught, the way she'd
been last year, trying to do a month's work in three or
four days. With the help of coffee, and by going without
sleep, she'd managed. But never again. The seniors, of
course, got a whole month off to do theses in their
majors, but Helena was a sophomore, and had to manage all her other subjects and continue classes as well.
Not, she admitted to herself, that I'd *want* to be stuck
with one of those senior theses. From the sound of some
of them, they might be doctors' degrees the kids were
after.

She collected the pile of books, returned them to the
desk, and paused for a word with the librarian, who
seemed to know every word written since the Rosetta
stone was hacked out.

"Any of those help you, Miss Williams?" the librarian asked, after a quick check of the titles, making sure they had all been returned.

"Gosh, yes, Mrs. Powell. Mostly, of course, I just made a list of what I'll be needing. But I took a few notes. And I'd like to take those—" she indicated two volumes "—with me."

Mrs. Powell handed her a couple of withdrawal slips. "Get them while you can. Pretty soon the seniors will be digging in for their thirty days' labor, and the rest of you will be lucky to find anything you want at all."

Helena smiled, took her books, and went down the marble corridor toward the entrance of the library. On the steps just outside, she paused. While she'd been studying, it had begun to snow, and the sky was filled now with a twisting tracery of white. The iron statue of Epke Banta Newell, long-ago founder of this very Newell College, donor of his name to this town of Newellton, was delicately powdered as it stood eternal guard in the quadrangle that lay between the library, the school buildings, the huge new gymnasium and swimming pool building. Epke Banta Newell's metal cape blew behind him, his metal face lifted itself to the falling flakes, and, as Helena watched, his outstretched palm collected a little mound of snow.

Hail, she said inwardly, as she often did, and then, as she often did, felt a little foolish. Still, from all she'd read, he seemed to have been a good enough old boy, and he *had* founded Newell College. Not that he'd ever intended it to enfold and cater to anything so unseemly as female educatees. Epke Banta Newell's college had been designed for the education and proper instruction of young gentlemen, and young ladies stayed at home doing petit point in the parlor, waiting.

Well, things have changed, she told him, going by, noticing that his buckled shoes were now well whitened, too. Your ideas about women are as obsolete as your buckled shoes. She did rather regret the shoes.

She walked on, a wonderfully warmed creature—beaver coat, red wool earmuffs and knee socks, thick mittens, straight tweed skirt—who resembled a college girl of a department store's dream, yet managed to invest the whole with her own light touch. Her walk, her swinging hair, the good humor of her admiration of Epke Banta Newell, for the college, for the town.

And the college *was* the town, even for those who never set foot within its classrooms. On the streets, in the shops, in the theater and inn, the college people, with their special clothes and their special language and their (presumably) special destinations, were the visible representation of what this particular spot in the world was about. College banners and mascots and blazers and beanies filled the shops. College announcements were on the billboards of the public library and inn, and the whole town (nearly the whole town) turned out for college athletic events, and really cared who won.

A college town, and divided between the town people and the college people, interdependent, but separated. Even those college students who had gone to high school here became, unintentionally sometimes, but inexorably, members of the latter class, especially if they lived not at home but in one of the sorority or fraternity buildings on the campus. People who had been friends in high school and truly meant to remain friends found through the chemistry of time, and a difference in the way in which it was spent, that they had less and less and finally nothing to say to each other. Boys who had played football together, studied together, dated together, only a few short years before, met on the street and wondered what to say.

"How's classes, Joe? Learning anything?"

"Sure enough. How's the garage? They work you hard?"

"Yup. The original grease monkey, that's me."

They grin, and silence falls.

"Well, good to see you again."

"Same here, boy. Same here."

"See you around?"

"Sure thing."

"Well . . . so long, then. Gotta be getting along."

"Yeah. So long. See you around."

Girls who had giggled all night together on pajama parties looked at each other and looked away. They couldn't talk about college without sounding as though one had made out better, gotten something better, than the other. They couldn't go back to the old high school days without seeming to emphasize that that was all they had in common. So they smiled vaguely, talked vaguely, went their ways.

Helena was one of those who had grown up in the town and now lived in its center, in a sorority house on the campus. She loved her life there, loved the college, her classes, her friends. She went home, to the large house across town, every other week end, and loved that, too. She was, in fact, a happy person. Yet she regretted, without knowing what to do about it, certain of her old friends, who thought, no doubt, that she'd become a snob, that she no longer cared about them. It wasn't true, and yet . . . and yet, it had happened. Last year, when she'd invited Phyllis Bookman for tea at the sorority house, what had they done? Reminisced a little, fallen silent, begun nervously to speak again, and recognized, before they parted, an unspoken defeat. They'd grown apart. Phyllis had attempted, just once, and delicately, to ask Helena to get her a blind date, but Helena had pretended not to understand. It wasn't very nice, but it was the way things were.

Helena, walking along in the ever-thickening snow, frowned a little as she thought of this, but imperceptibly other matters took possession of her mind, and when she reached the house, she'd forgotten about it. She shivered a little, coming into the warmth and gentle light of the hallway, and as she climbed the stairs began pulling off her coat.

Roxanne Howells, her roommate, folded like a nicely proportioned giraffe in the room's only good chair, glanced up as Helena entered. "Cold?" she asked in the comfortable tones of one who hasn't known the cold for hours.

"Mmm. Funny how you don't know how really cold it is until you get out of it." Helena hung up her coat, removed her earmuffs, walked to the dresser, and picked up her comb. "Anyone call?" she asked, arranging her hair. She crossed to her desk, eyed the two books she'd brought from the library, and glanced over at Roxanne. "I said, did anyone call?"

"Heard you."

"Well?"

Roxanne shrugged. "I wasn't supposed to say, but Jay Etting called and said he'd be over here at nine o'clock. Says since you won't answer his letters or his phone calls, he's going to sit downstairs until you're in disgrace with the housemother. Says we'll have to call bouncers to eject him." Roxanne delivered this message with a straight face, and then began to smile. "He sounded awfully sincere, Helena. Why don't you give him a break? After all, everyone's entitled to mistakes."

Helena sat down and rested her chin on her fist with an exasperated sigh. "I don't care how many mistakes Jay Etting makes. Just so they have nothing to do with me."

"But it certainly isn't like you to be so . . . sulky and relentless."

"I am *not*. And I wish to heaven people would stop treating this—this business between Jay and me as if it were a lovers' quarrel and they were divinely appointed to smooth it out. I was never in love with him and I'm not trying to punish him. I'm only trying not to see him any more."

"But you were going with him practically steady before that silly Thanksgiving Dance fiasco."

"I know I was. But whether or not anyone believes it, and, mind you, I don't *care* whether or not they believe it, it was just a sort of habit. I wasn't in love with him, except maybe at the very beginning. And besides, Roxanne, that—that Rosemary Reed wasn't the only girl he flirted with. I mean, not that it isn't perfectly all right to flirt, but you know quite as well as I do that Jay can't resist *any* pretty girl. I used to be positively humiliated at the way he behaved when we were out. Whispering with other girls, holding their hands, right in front of my eyes. And pretending it was all so comradely. It got boring, and I was really sort of glad to find out about how he'd taken somebody from the town out the minute I left to visit my cousin."

"My, my. And you the one who always complains about the snobbery of saying town girl."

"All right," Helena admitted after a pause. "You win. It wasn't a pretty remark. But it just happens—"

"Just happens?" Roxanne encouraged.

"Well, it just happens that that particular girl is one I never liked to start with. And it also just happens that I mentioned it to Jay after we'd met her. She was boy crazy in high school, and a mantrap who didn't care who got hurt, just so she got what she wanted. And got it," Helena added dryly, "just about every time she chose."

"Get something of yours?" Roxanne inquired.

"Yes. A boy I really liked, too. The only one, I suppose, I ever really liked." She lifted her head a little and her face took on a remote cast as she returned to a past time, a time when she had not known Roxanne but had known, only too well, a girl named Rosemary and an icy, frightening conviction that no matter what she did this first deep love was going to be taken from her. She had tried, oh how desperately she had tried, to hold him, and all her trying had only made Rosemary's conquest easier.

"What happened to him?" Roxanne asked.

Helena sighed and returned to the present. "I don't know. Moved away, to some other part of the country. I really hadn't thought about him in ages, and now I don't suppose I really care." She thought about that a moment. "No, I honestly don't. But, you see, it didn't help to have Jay go hotfooting it back to Rosemary Reed the minute my back was turned."

"What did you tell him about her?"

"I don't remember. Oh, that I didn't care for her much, something like that."

"In what tone of voice?"

"How should I know?"

"I can guess. You said it in the tone that meant Miss Reed was a mantrap and boy crazy."

"So that's why he went back, you mean?"

"It's possible."

"Probable, you mean. Well, it doesn't endear Jay to me, and doesn't make me anything but annoyed at this silly notion of his about hanging around here."

"Maybe you're being prudish," Roxanne suggested slyly.

"Prudish? What do you mean, prudish? What has—"

"I mean," Roxanne interrupted, "that, after all, boys

get to a certain age and there are certain things they want that they don't get from nice girls, so—" She shrugged. "Quite a natural development, I believe."

"Oh, for heaven's sake, Roxanne, you sound like a Kinsey report, and that's the worst kind of snob remark I've ever heard you make. Just because I don't like her doesn't mean Rosemary isn't what you call a *nice* girl. It happens that she is. Being boy crazy is one thing, and being promiscuous is quite another. I know her well enough to know she never had to be promiscuous, and I also know she's well brought up. You should be ashamed."

Roxanne unfolded her long legs and arms, stretched, and then admitted that perhaps she was. "Stupid thing to say," she mumbled. "I'd simply like to add that I don't think you should hold it against Jay that—"

"I know, I know. We all make mistakes. Look, Roxanne, this conversation wearies me, so let's drop it, all right?"

"Whatever you say." Roxanne gathered soap dish and towel. "I'm going to take a bath," she said, standing at the door. "Are you going to see Jay tonight? Or wait for Mrs. Mack to call the bouncers?"

Helena bit her lip. "See him, I suppose. He'd never mind causing a ruckus, and he knows it would drive me crazy. Oh, *really*."

Roxanne left the room.

When she had gone, Helena paced about, fell into the big chair, and stared at her desk. She didn't want to see Jay Etting, and, no matter what anyone thought, it was not because she was angry or hurt. She'd been embarrassed when she heard about his taking Rosemary to the dance, but anger and hurt had vanished quickly, leaving a residue of vexation and a large measure of relief at having a good excuse to get out of seeing him any more. He was—he was too importunate, too difficult to handle. He was a miracle of self-concern. And he was, as she'd told Roxanne, as girl crazy as Rosemary had ever been boy crazy.

She had liked Jay once. More than she'd admit to Roxanne or anyone else. She'd nearly admitted it to Jay himself, and that would have been a mistake. But her affection had taken a series of jolts. She'd been stood up several times, had watched while Jay flirted across a dance floor, across a ballpark, practically (he had such good eyesight where girls were concerned), and had been, for a time, convinced when he swore that he couldn't help the broken date ("I could *not* get to a phone. This guy's nose was bleeding all over the place and I had to get him to the infirmary." . . . "I swear, Helena, I was studying so blasted hard and by the time I looked at the clock—" . . . "But my *mother* turned up, and before I could say a thing, she had me in the car and off to dinner somewhere. My lord, you don't think I *wanted* to stand you up?"); had believed him when he would turn to her in astonishment and say, "What girl? I wasn't looking at any girl. There's a fellow over there I used to know and I was trying to catch his eye, is all." Yes, she'd endured it for a long time, but the deepest love could not survive such trials, and, Helena admitted, her love had been not so much deep as turbulent. Jay was very handsome, and the touch of his hand a sensation she could still recall with a tingling start. But he was unreliable and unspeakably selfish, and she no longer cared about him one way or the other.

He would, however, be difficult to convince. His self-esteem was involved in this, and Jay took devoted care of his self-esteem. Helena, absently picking up a pencil to chew on, set about devising a way to convince him. It had better be good, she thought. It had better be awfully good.

Chapter Three

ROSEMARY REED PUT THE NEWSPAPER ON THE TABLE beside her father's chair, glanced around the living room restlessly, sighed, and went into the kitchen, where Lenore was preparing dinner. Lenore hummed as she worked, pouring cream of mushroom soup over a mixture of tuna fish and noodles, sprinkling breadcrumbs and bits of oleomargarine over the top, stepping back to view the effect with the critical eye of a creator.

"You'd think it was roast suckling pig," Rosemary said, trying not to sound irritated.

"Oh, spare me that. Did the ad get in the paper?"

"Why not?" Rosemary shrugged. "Sure, it's there. And pretty soon the telephone will ring and some drip will announce that she's a student at the college and she read our ad and has the room been taken yet, please, and how much and how big and how good are the breakfasts—" She broke off, began to gather silver and dishes to set the table.

"You're getting frown lines, sweetie," Lenore said. She

41

slid the tuna concoction into the oven. "Anyway, what's wrong with all that? They have to ask questions, and it's natural to say you're a student, if you are one. I suppose it is. I know *I* would."

They looked at each other with comprehension and without words. Neither of them could possibly attend college, a fact they'd always known and to which they had never been resigned. Rosemary, now twenty, had become rather bitter about it. Lenore, a senior in high school, had a wistful way of mentioning the college. Only once had they asked their father if it were possible for them to become a part of that privileged, blissful, greatly to be wished for world. That had been when Rosemary was in her last year of school, and Mr. Reed, turning grumpy as he generally did when refusing things, said, "Forget it. You're lucky to get through high school." Rosemary considered that an unfair remark. They weren't lucky to get through high school, it was their right, and Pop knew it as well as they did. But she didn't argue, because Pop had never been known to change his mind about anything. So, though they did not forget it, they accepted the fact that for them the college might just as well not exist.

"In fact," Rosemary said now, "I wish to heaven we lived in some other town. Any place at all, just so it didn't have a college in it. I wish we lived in a town that didn't even have a grammar school, and then *we* could feel superior."

"I don't want to feel superior," Lenore said. "I'd just sort of like to . . ."

"To what?"

"To learn a little more, maybe."

"Oh—*learn*," Rosemary said with scorn. "That's all very fine, but I wanted to go so those darn college girls couldn't turn their noses up at me." And so college boys, she thought, from a depth of painful remembrance, couldn't humiliate me. She did not mention that to Lenore, who was saying that she didn't think the college girls turned their noses up. "It's more that they don't notice us at all," she said with a wry smile.

"That's worse," Rosemary cried desperately, and then, with an elaborate gesture, dismissed the topic. "Your creation, Oscar, smells divine. I trust you did not forget the truffles?"

"Forget the *truffles*, madame? Why I rooted them out myself. Can't trust these modern pigs to know a truffle from a toadstool. Things were different, let me tell you, when *I* was a boy."

They grinned at each other and then started slightly as the kitchen door opened and Mr. Reed came in, rubbing his hands together and then cupping them over his ears.

"Twelve above," he informed them with an aggrieved air. "Dinner will have to be rushed. That infernal *helper* of mine has to get off early tonight because his mother is sick, he *says.*"

Washing his hands under the kitchen faucet, he took a moment to glance dismally at Rosemary. It was the one matter in which his entreaties and demands had gotten him nowhere, this of having Rosemary work in the department store rather than in her father's small candy store. She'd done it afternoons and week ends all through high school, hadn't she? Then why the devil not now, when she could work full time and really be of some help? Nervous, unhappy, but adamant, Rosemary had refused, and had gotten herself a job the day following graduation. Pop could not conceive, could never believe had she told him, how she loathed that candy store. How the cramped duskiness of it, the dusty shelves of cheap and foolish and often vulgar notions, the spigots dispensing soft drinks, the wells containing ice cream, the stacks of paper books and pencil boxes and notebooks and magazines, the jacks and the chocolate cigarettes and the comics lay upon her spirits as if they all were stone. And how—oh, above all—how she stiffened when the college students came in—for magazines or reprints only—and didn't even see her as they said, "No *Roget's Thesaurus?* Oh yes, here it is," and handed her thirty-five cents and went out in the sunshine again.

"I can't," she'd said over and over. "Pop, I just cannot." And ultimately, astounded and outraged, he'd realized that she would not. He'd had a succession of part-time helpers. People who'd mind the store while he hurried home for lunch, for dinner. Currently it was a frail boy of seventeen who worried about his complexion, who discouraged it by helping himself to penny candies and soft drinks, who looked, and was, as unreliable as a drifting straw. "Kids don't take their responsibilities seriously any more at all," Mr. Reed said now, pulling a chair up to the kitchen table. "Let me tell you, things were different when *I* was a boy."

Lenore and Rosemary did not risk glancing at each other. He *would* say precisely what they expected him to say.

"Maybe his mother really is sick," Lenore said, putting a plate of tuna-noodle casserole, boiled carrots, and buttered bread before her father.

Mr. Reed did not reply, and for a while they ate in silence. It was dark, the early dark of midwinter. The night stood frigid against the windowpanes and a small draft sidled beneath the kitchen door and spread over the thin linoleum. They ate, and now and then, from beneath lowered lids, Rosemary studied her only two relatives.

Mother had said once that she and Lenore looked alike, except that Lenore was tranquil and Rosemary was agitated. That was just a way of talking, really, but there was some truth in it. They were not very tall, but had lovely figures and they carried themselves well. Mother had taught them to do that. "Those girls in the movies *walk* tall," she'd told them. "That's what makes them look so elegant." And so Lenore and Rosemary began to walk tall, and still did. They both had brown eyes, but where Lenore's were a golden brown, Rosemary's were almost black. Rosemary, she knew it herself, had nicer eyes. Dark brown and sparkling, deep-set, with thick black lashes, they made her almost a person of beauty. But Lenore, she thought often, has beauty of expression; that mildness and dearness that is in her face is beauty. Rosemary was too restless, too discontented, to be beautiful. Yet the high school yearbook had referred to them as "the stunning Reed sisters." They had liked that. Even Pop had smiled.

Sometimes it seemed as though they three had always been together, with no mother, no aunts and cousins coming to call, no contact with the world at all. Since their mother had died and the relations on her side had dispersed to other parts of the country, it had been like that—James Reed and his two daughters, and the boarder who was always—nearly always—with them, but who never shared anything of their lives but the room paid for. The last one had been a gym teacher from the high school, a woman who pranced and called hearty greetings but firmly refused to do more than greet and run. Not that Lenore and Rosemary had minded. "She'd have us doing pushups and chinning ourselves on the towel racks, if we let her," Rosemary said. The fact that they both knew the gym teacher didn't care at all what they did was immaterial. The remark made them feel feminine and superior. When the gym teacher announced, at the end of last term, that she was leaving to be married, the two girls had felt deceived and betrayed. "Married?" Rosemary had shrieked, watching the stocky form of their boarder go bounding down the icy streets toward her final class. "Why it'll take a weight-lifter to carry her over the threshold." The remark had been pure bluster and helped not at all. The gym teacher was marrying, leaving her job, going to live in California. The gym teacher had accomplished everything, and making fun of her only made fools of them. They cleaned out her room, spent Christmas with just the three of them, and now it was a new semester, a new year, their ad was in the paper, and it was all to do again. Rosemary sighed, met her father's glance, and turned from it.

After dinner Mr. Reed shoveled coal into the furnace before returning to the shop to release his helper. Rosemary did the dishes. Lenore did her homework. An evening like any other. Presently Hank Shipman, Lenore's devoted steady, would put in his nightly appearance, and he and Lenore would sit together in the living room, listening to Hank's records, talking softly, looking at each other with love and ardor. And later, after Pop had come in and gone to his early bed, Hank and Lenore would turn off all the lights but one dim one, and . . . well, the word, Rosemary said to herself, is neck. Yet you could trust them, those two very much in love but serene and stable people. You knew that Hank would never hurt his Lenore, and you knew that Lenore's particular sort of reserve would always protect her. Younger than I am, Rosemary thought, but she's always been smarter, and cooler, and—nicer. Lenore had never been described by that hateful term, boy crazy. A term that even now made Rosemary uneasy and a little ashamed, though certainly she had never done anything shameful. Only gotten crushes, in a silly, fitful way, on this one and that for reasons that she knew herself were not too substantial. Because of a beautifully shaped arm, a nice turn of speech, an accidental meeting of the eyes.

Oh, her years had been one long series of crushes—and often conquests—that had not been very satisfying, which she had been unable to resist. But that was over now. Quite completely over, she told herself rigidly, and there was no reason to burn at sudden recollections the way she did, no reason at all to duck her head against the memory of just a little too much petting, a little too much disregard of other girls' feelings. It was over.

It had taken, something within her reminded unpleasantly, just one lopsided grin from Jay Etting to arouse the old response. Lenore would never be so changeable, so easily suggestible. Lenore didn't have the sort of confused and hungry mind that dupes its owner and leads her into shabby situations. Rosemary wrung out the dishcloth as though it were a small, loathed life, as though it were a memory she could throttle, and then, with deliberation, carefully wiped the drainboard and table, turned off the kitchen light, and went into the living room.

"How're you coming?" she asked her sister.

Lenore closed her books. "All done." She indicated a slim blue volume. "When we got that *Crime de Sylvestre Bonnard,* I thought we were going to have a mystery in French. Crimers. Do you have a date, or anything?"

"Reg is driving upstate tonight. He won't be back till tomorrow."

"Oh. Don't you get worried about him, Rosemary?"

"Worried?"

"I mean, driving on nights like this? It's awfully cold and icy. Gosh, if Hank were driving anywhere at all, much less a couple of hundred miles, I'd worry all right."

"Reg knows what he's doing. He's been driving that thing for years."

"Three years," Lenore said. She was fond of Reg Erskine, who drove a truck, saved his money, loved Rosemary devotedly. If I could feel about Reg the way Lenore feels about Hank, Rosemary thought, I'd do it with rapture. And heaven knew, she'd tried. She supposed she loved him. How could you not love someone who loved you as Reg did her? Who was handsome and gentle and enormously strong, and who had ambition. Reg did not intend to be a truck driver all his days. He was going to be, he told them, an owner of trucks. Of a fleet of trucks. Lenore and Rosemary believed him, because it was impossible to believe that Reg would not do anything he'd made up his mind to. Except, Rosemary reminded herself marry me. He hasn't been able to do that. He hadn't even put it in clear words yet, being too canny to risk an early refusal. But she knew what he wanted. Only how could she marry a man when the feelings he summoned up in her were gratitude, peacefulness, and the sort of affectionate love that you'd give to anyone as fine as Reg when you knew him well? Rosemary wanted not just to love, but to be *in* love, to be lost and drowned, heedless and reckless.

She got up abruptly and went to the hall closet for her coat and boots. Lenore glanced up disapprovingly. "Where are you going?"

"For a walk."

"A walk?" She glanced at the window. "It's beginning to snow. It's cold out."

"That's fine. You aren't going anywhere, are you? You and Hank?"

"Heck, no. Why?"

"In case someone calls about the room."

"Funny nobody's called yet."

Rosemary tied a scarf around her head. "Wouldn't be as many calls this time of year, I suppose. Most people got themselves settled in the fall. Maybe we won't get anyone at all," she added hopefully, and subsided at Lenore's, "We'd darn well better, or there won't be any tuna fish, much less truffles, in the noodles." There could be only agreement with that remark, and Rosemary, going outside, acknowledged it despondently. They were lucky to have the extra room and bath, and they *had* to rent it. She remembered how excited she'd been, when they'd moved here, to find an entire extra bathroom. It led off what the real estate man had called "the master bedroom." To have both a master bedroom and two bathrooms had seemed almost too opulent and Rosemary became so overwrought that her mother had had to speak very sharply. Still, Pop, thumbs in the armholes of his vest (it had been summer when they'd moved), had nodded with satisfaction. "High class," he'd said. "Pretty darn high class." It wasn't, Rosemary had come to know. It was just a house that had an extra bathroom, a leaking roof, deficient plumbing, and no insulation. The roof and the plumbing problems had been remedied, with moaning and expense. The insulation kept them uncomfortable winter and summer. When Mom had died, living expenses had gone up, and Pop moved out of the master bedroom to make space for the first of many lodgers. There'd been men, women, an occasional college student. Rosemary and Lenore kept the room clean, provided the breakfast, and ceased at last even to resent the strangers who came and went. They were no part of the Reeds' life, but only contributed something to make that life a bit less harsh.

Taking deep breaths of the bitter, piercing air, Rosemary walked quickly toward the drugstore that glowed on a corner four blocks away. The snow grew denser by the moment and at this rate would require shoveling by morning. But it was very lovely. The large flakes coming to rest on her clothes, her lashes, gradually whitening the sidewalks, sifting against the houses. Even this dispirited street, composed of old untended houses and stores that had pretensions not even to neatness, became somehow transformed when the snow fell. I suppose, Rosemary told herself, because the snow obscures it somewhat. When Rosemary was hurt, she always took refuge in cynicism, while her father grew grumpy, and Lenore wistful. Lenore came out of this best, her sister thought. Pop had a reputation for sullenness, because he was so frequently baffled and discouraged that his bad temper showed more often than his good. And Rosemary herself seemed rather a hard person, too suspicious, too self-motivated. Since the night Jay Etting had taken her out, she'd been so brooding and withdrawn that even her father had reproved her, saying, "You're getting sort of—tough, or something, Rosie. It isn't nice in a girl." Tough, Rosemary repeated to herself now, and her hands in her pockets clenched into tight fists. Tough. And I was so naive, so eager. So dumb.

She walked through the snow, not wanting to remember, but remembering, and at the drugstore hesitated a moment before she turned in.

"Hot chocolate, please," she asked the woman behind the soda fountain. "With a lot of whipped cream."

The stout attendant shook her head as she prepared the rich drink. "You girls," she said. "You just don't know how lucky you are." She seemed happy over Rosemary's luck.

Rosemary sipped the scalding drink carefully, and carefully spooned the airy froth of whipped cream into her mouth. It tasted good, on a night so cold. The drugstore was nice, warm and lighted. There were lots of things to enjoy. And perhaps, when more months had added themselves to the months already past, she would forget, or be able to call it experience. She closed her eyes against the recollection, opened them deliberately, and looked around the drugstore. There were at least ten people in it, and all of them had problems they'd learned to live with. That's really what it comes to, maybe, she decided. Not so much forgetting them, as living with them, learning something from them. She'd been . . . she'd been made a fool of. Well, she still had Lenore, and Reg, and she was able to eat whipped cream without worrying.

"I suppose I am," she said to the stout woman. "In lots of ways."

"How's that?"

"Lucky," said Rosemary. "Like you said."

At about the time Rosemary began her walk, Jay Etting arrived at Helena's sorority house, began to give a gay eye to the girl who opened the door to him, remembered what he was there for, and sobered quickly.

"I would like to see Helena Williams," he said solemnly as an applicant for a loan. "That is, if she's in?" And if she were not, he'd wait. He kept his face grave, despite the minxlike glance the little blonde tossed at him, and followed her into the living room.

"I'll give her a call," the blonde said, withdrawing her minx glance as apparently wasted in this situation.

Jay nodded his thanks and settled in the corner of a sofa by the wall. He glanced around the room. Chintzy, like all these houses. Very cheerful. It was one of the best on campus, and had, so far as Jay was concerned, about the best-looking girls. Well-to-do, most of them, and well cherished. Shining hair, nice complexions, pretty clothes. He'd been ten sorts of a fool to risk losing Helena for a chance reaction to Rosemary Reed, who'd given him the high sign in the store that day, all right. Somehow he had to respond to high signs, if the girls were attractive. A disease, he'd been telling himself for weeks. I've got a sort of weakness, and Helena's just going to have to help me recover. He rather liked that notion. Now, let's see . . . how could he best phrase it? *Look, dearest, darling Helena*— No, that sounded a little excessive. *Helena, it comes to this*— Nope, too businesslike. *Helena, believe me*— That was better. *Believe me, when I say to you*—

"Well, Jay? Here I am."

He bounded to his feet, the lopsided smile coming

with warmth and naturalness. "Gosh, Helena. Oh gosh, it's good to see you." He attempted to take her hand, desisted quickly. "Come, sit here and we can talk."

Helena glanced around the fairly occupied living room. "Talk about what?" she said, adding, "I only came down because Roxanne said you'd made all sorts of silly threats to embarrass me if I didn't." She remained standing.

"Ah, Helena, baby, I didn't mean to embarrass you. I just meant I had to see you, and you've been so darned stuck-up—"

"Not stuck-up. Fed up. And if you'd like to know, you're embarrassing me right now." She spoke in a near whisper, and Jay became aware of covert and amused glances from others in the room. "What did you want?" Helena asked.

"You're making it awfully hard."

"You started it. And I have no intention of making it easy, but I'd like to make it quick."

"Look, would you take a walk with me? Not far, just so we can—can talk in privacy? Please, Helena, I want it very much."

You want so much very much, Helena thought, and was surprised at herself for not yielding to the old charm of his looks, his manner. It was one of the reasons she'd avoided him, the fear of being enmeshed despite herself. Now here she was, talking to him coolly, indifferent to his wants (except that they might make her ridiculous in the eyes of the girls and other couples here), and his looks were . . . Just his looks. Very splendid. Nothing to brood over, sigh over. Nothing to cry over. I remember when I used to cry over him, she thought curiously. How could I have? "All right," she said. "I'll get my coat."

When they were outside, in the swirling snow that now shrouded the streets, they walked a block or two not speaking. Helena noticed how they still managed to keep step with each other. It was one of the things Jay had first commented on when they met. "Why is it that girls have such trouble keeping step with people?" he'd asked, and then smiled sideways at Helena beside him. "Walking with you is like walking with my shadow," he told her. And Helena had been jubilant at the praise. She remembered it now with faint incredulity.

Jay said, "See, you're still the only girl who knows how to walk properly."

How many have you been walking with since last fall? Helena wondered. She did not ask, knowing Jay would interpret jealousy whether or not there was any.

"Aren't you going to speak at all?" he asked.

"Why do you assume people have to keep step with you? Did you ever try fitting your steps to someone else's?" Jay looked baffled. "It's not important, and I only said it to try to point out something to you *about* you. If people keep in step with you, they're to be praised; and if they don't, then they're the ones who are out of step."

"Oh now, it isn't that way at all," he began, and did not continue.

"What way is it?" she asked after a while.

Jay lifted his snow-dusted shoulders. "Dunno, as a

matter of fact. Maybe you're right." At Helena's dubious expression, he added, "No, I'm serious. I just—never thought of it before. Not that I haven't been doing a heck of a lot of thinking in the past couple of months." He slid her an appraising glance, but Helena, lifting her face to the snow, was inscrutable. "I suppose you don't care, and maybe you won't let me see you again, but I had to tell you this once that the whole thing was—just a thing. One of those things. Didn't mean beans to me, any part of it, and I sure never expected you to go into a tailspin like this. Oh, I knew you'd be sore, but, my gosh, girl, you can't shackle a guy to his room, just be-cause—"

"I had no wish to shackle you. Then or now," she said firmly.

"Okay. Punish me. If it makes you feel better, go ahead and punish me."

He just can't bear, Helena thought, to give up any-thing he once considered his. She halted suddenly, turned to face him. "Jay, I wonder why you can't get it through your head that I have no wish to punish you, or do anything else about you. I have—no desires any way at all where you're concerned. But as long as you had to start this, I don't mind telling you, once again, something I tried to tell you a few minutes ago. *You are conceited.*" She said the last three words slowly and distinctly, preventing him with her eyes from interrupt-ing. "Monstrously conceited. You take everything any-body does as directed toward you, in some way con-cerned with you. The smallest remark doesn't seem to have a point until you've considered how it relates to you. And I think that if you're ever going to grow up, or have a—a reasonable, decent relationship with people, you've got to start forgetting yourself. You remind me of a little child, only there's an excuse for them. People who've grown up begin to notice that they're sharing the world with other people, and all roads don't lead to sonny. You think I'm angry about Rosemary Reed, and I was, I suppose, at the time—"

"I tell you, she didn't mean a thing to me."

"—at the time," Helena continued. "But I wasn't for long, and I got over it *completely*. And do you actually think that saying she didn't mean a thing to you helps matters? You poor ninny, that makes it worse than ever." She stood with her hands on her hips, glaring up at him.

He leaned over and kissed the tip of her nose. "I adore you when you're angry," he said.

Helena felt smothered with annoyance. Was there no way to make him understand? "I'm going back, Jay," she told him. "This is just silly."

As she turned, he put a detaining hand on her arm. "Helena, please." There was an unusual note of pleading in his voice. "Come on and have a cup of coffee or something with me, and we'll talk."

"We don't have anything to talk about."

"Yes. Or, at least, I do. You said you'd— Come on, just for a little while."

Sighing a little, she resumed her pace beside him, and presently they came to a drugstore and turned in just as Rosemary slid off a stool at the soda fountain. The three stood staring at each other for a surprised moment, and then Rosemary, with a peculiar little ducking nod, her cheeks reddened, hurried past them into the cold.

"Well," said Jay, looking after her. "That was—" He didn't seem to know what it was. Helena wasn't sure either. It was—what? A little sad, she decided wearily. Rosemary, in her somewhat shabby clothes, her color heightened, giving that bob of recognition and going off alone seemed, to Helena's bemusement, a touching figure. Oh, for the love of heaven, she said to herself, I sound like a trailer for *East Lynne*. She shook her head, walked to a booth, and sat down without waiting for Jay.

"You see, you're still annoyed," he said, as he slid to the bench opposite. There was more than a trace of smugness in his voice. "It still gets you down, the thought of Rosemary Re—"

"You bore me, Jay. If you have something to say, get along with it, so I can go home."

They ordered coffee, and when it came Jay set his aside impatiently, as though too intent on his purpose to allow petty distractions. "Helena," he said, "I've never cared for any girl the way I care for you. Never." He said this, and waited for her moved response. When she gave him none at all, he leaned forward urgently, one hand flat on the table top, the other brushing his hair back. "You've got to believe me. All those—I mean, any other girls I went around with were just . . . oh, pastimes. When you were away, or had another date, or something. And speaking of that, I never took a nosedive or complained around and refused to see you when *you* had dates."

"You wouldn't have had a right to."

"But then neither do you."

Taking a deep breath, Helena fixed her eyes on him. "All right, now. I'll try to say this once again, and then I'm going to finish my coffee and go home. I did not go into a tailspin, take a nosedive, complain around, or refuse to see you because you took another girl out. It was partly because it was Rosemary Reed, that particular girl, as I think I mentioned to you before (although, she thought, just that brief encounter had strangely changed her attitude about Rosemary. I don't like her any better, she realized, nor have any wish to know her better, but she's different from what she was in school, subdued, not the way I described her to Roxanne. In a baffling way, this was not satisfactory). There's something else," she went on to Jay, "and the something else is far more important. I got sick and tired of your whole attitude, and if you want to know, I was rather relieved when you took her out, because it gave me an excuse to break off with you."

That was unkind, she told herself, but would not have taken the words back.

"You don't mean that," Jay said soberly. "Your pride's been hurt, and that's a tough thing to bear. But I tell you, I'm finished with other girls. After this, it's me and you, Helena, for good."

She looked at him in total astonishment, her mouth open, her eyebrows drawn in dumbfounded curves. The urge to laugh was put down with difficulty. "Are you proposing to me?" she managed at last.

"Huh? Oh, no, for lord's sake. I mean, that isn't what

I mean . . . That is, the lord's sake part of it. I mean, I don't mean I wouldn't like . . . or that maybe some day . . . But cripes, Helena, I've gotta finish college, and all—"

She regarded him steadily, and only her lips quivered a little. She made no gesture to help him out.

"What I meant was, for the rest of college. You and me, steady. Okay? And afterward . . . Well, I wouldn't be at all surprised if—" He broke off, but gave her a heavily significant nod. "So—" he put a hand on hers "—that's all set, isn't it?"

"What is? That we'll get married after college?"

He jumped back with something close to alarm, then relaxed as Helena allowed her laughter to escape. "Oh, kidding me, are you? Well, you just wait and see, it may turn out not to be a kidding matter after all." He seemed, suddenly, to consider that remark imprudent, and hurried on. "How about tomorrow night, is it a date?"

Helena shook her head. "Sorry. All booked up for quite a while."

"Going to make it hard for me?" he said, with something like indulgence. "Well, when then?"

"I guess you'd better call."

"Have to consult your book?"

"Perhaps."

He seemed determined to see this through. But not, Helena told herself, for my sake. For his own. For that pride of his that won't take no. "You call me," she repeated, and they rose.

Back in her room, she found Roxanne unreasonably

enjoying a trigonometry problem, but willing to abandon it for conversation. "They're practically taking odds downstairs," she informed Helena. "Will she, won't she, will she, won't she, date with Jay?"

"She's said yes, at any rate," Helena replied.

"No kidding?" Roxanne was distinctly surprised. "Well, I lose then. I'd have sworn you really meant it."

"Oh, you don't precisely lose," said Helena, rummaging for her curlers.

"Cryptic," Roxanne muttered. "Everybody's so darn cryptic." She swiveled about to face her roommate, and, when Helena pretended not to notice, said crisply, "Now, come on. Tell Mama all about it."

Helena shook her head, smiling a little. "My plans are not sufficiently matured. But you'll know, in time."

"In time for what?"

"Not in time *for* anything. Just in time, in a measure, degree, place in time. What a mixed-up language English is. No precision. For instance, if I say a thing is not, clearly, in sight . . . do I mean it's clearly not in sight, or not clearly in sight?"

"Nothing's clear to me at all," Roxanne said. "And of course I *had* to say that, after what you'd said, didn't I?"

Helena nodded. "Isn't that peculiar? You know, Roxanne, I think it might be interesting to do a paper on it. Let's both do one, not consulting, and see what we get."

Roxanne, sitting up alertly, said, "That'd be great. We can do them independently and then give them to Mr. Warner and tell him what we—"

"But not in a hurry, mind," Helena interrupted. "We'll

have to take our time, and maybe make them our term papers. And *don't* let Anne McGinnis know. She's too word-conscious as it is. She'd muscle in, and three would be too many."

"No. No McGinnis," Roxanne agreed. They talked quickly, interrupting each other again and again, about the possibilities before them, and Jay Etting had quite slipped their minds.

CHAPTER FOUR

"ROOM'S TAKEN," MR. REED SAID AT DINNER. HE POURED catsup on his canned hash, looked at the result without interest, and began to eat.

Lenore and Rosemary exchanged a surprised look.

"Taken?" said Lenore. "Taken when?"

"Lunchtime. Young fellow from the college came around. Said he wanted a room for a month, so's to work on his—theme?" Mr. Reed offered doubtfully. "It was something like that."

"Thesis?" Lenore asked.

Mr. Reed nodded. "That's it."

"Why did you rent it for a month, Pop?" Rosemary asked. "We'll only have to run the ad again and start from the beginning. And why . . . I mean, where is he now that he can't do his thesis there?"

"I rented it," her father said heavily, "because we didn't get another call in the whole week. Lose the price of the ad just waiting, wouldn't we? And he lives in one of the fraternity houses. Too much noise and goings on to work properly, he says. He's a senior and looks steady enough." He fixed his two girls with an eye of belated warning, as though qualities other than steadiness might be apparent to them, where they had not to him. "I rented it because I had to," he repeated, "but don't you two go getting ideas."

Pop always described an action of which he might disapprove as getting ideas. When they were younger, if they mentioned a movie, or a dress, or an excursion to a nearby amusement park and Pop was unprepared to provide, he'd say, "Don't go getting ideas," before they'd actually made a request. And now he was warning them against any possible interest in the new boarder. He must, Rosemary decided, be rather anxious about money to accept a young man at all, and on a monthly basis. It worried her, but she knew better than to put a direct question to him. He never had admitted that by her working in the department store rather than for him they made out better financially, and he'd bristled like a porcupine on the few occasions when she'd suggested they work out a budget together. He gave them the house money, but Pop was head of the household, and as such admitted no interference or advice. Well, Rosemary thought, one thing he needn't worry over is *ideas* about the new lodger. Lenore wouldn't even know what he looked like, and she herself would never look at a college boy again. She squirmed, remembering the bad fortune of meeting Jay and Helena in the drugstore that night, remembering her own self-conscious flight and their air of surprise and constraint.

"When does he come?" she asked her father, trying to put the recollection from her.

"Tomorrow. Wants peace and quiet so's to work on this theme."

"Well, don't worry. He'll get it."

After dinner, while Lenore did the dishes, Rosemary gave the master bedroom a final cleaning, put fresh linen on the bed, a cotton runner with tatted edges on the bureau. She put towels and soap in the bathroom, found a few of the gym teacher's hairpins wedged behind the closet shelf when she lined it with fresh paper. Even the hairpins didn't make it seem as though the gym teacher had ever lived here. The room never conceded the existence of past boarders. It conceded, faintly, like an old fragrance, the long-ago presence of Mom and Pop and a house properly their own, a master bedroom properly itself. Rosemary put shelf paper in the bureau drawers, adjusted the blinds, glanced once more around the room, and went out, closing the door behind her.

Reg was in the living room when she came downstairs, long legs stretched out, head leaning against the back of the chair, eyes closed. He was, as he always was, tired, and one of the reasons Rosemary felt she was not really in love with him was that this did not annoy her. If she'd loved him, surely she'd have minded that he couldn't stay awake, even for her. That he fell asleep in movies, begged off taking her out in order to sit around the house drinking beer and talking or looking at television. If she'd loved him, she'd have wanted his attention, and as it was she merely felt sorry that he got so fatigued, and let him look at television all he wanted.

"Hi," he said now, opening his eyes and yawning

deeply. He did not get up from his chair, but grinned at her fondly and said, "Here's Hercules, all set to howl."

"Was it a bad trip?" she asked, sitting on the sofa and stifling the yawn he'd almost forced on her. Yawning was silly. Even a yawning cat could make you do likewise. She couldn't think of any other action that could duplicate itself on everyone around.

"Oh—good, bad. I dunno," said Reg. "They're all about the same. I put another fifty in the bank today."

"That's nice, Reg."

"Nice? That all you have to say? This brings it up to a clear two thousand. I sort of thought we'd celebrate. You realize that two thousand represents half what I'm aiming for? Another two and I can buy that truck and still have enough left over for—well, you know, furniture, stuff like that."

It was a funny kind of courtship, Reg's, but courtship it was. And there was another proof that her affection for him was almost sisterly. Because it had taken Reg three years and most of his time to save that money. Probably it would take him another three to double it. He'd never said so directly, but she knew that when the bank account showed four thousand, the possibility of buying the first of the trucks, Rosemary was going to be proposed to. Meanwhile he came as a matter of course to call on her when he was free, made elaborately offhand references to the purchase of furniture, took her to movies (or did not), bought her and Lenore and Pop modest presents at Christmastime, was welcomed as a dinner guest in the manner of a relative, and, when he kissed her, moved her to no feeling stronger than fondness. Lenore insisted that when the day came that he was able to marry her, Reg would be an entirely different person. "He respects you, Rosemary. That's why he's dull." Rosemary, laughing, said no doubt that was right. But when even Lenore, Reg's champion, admitted so innocently that he could be dull, what was the girl who was supposed to be in love to feel? *You be dull and kindly, for three years, dear, and then set me on fire.* It was too late now for Reg to set her heart pounding at the mere touch of his hand. And yet, she thought, looking at his tough, tired, strong face with its gentle eyes, I'd be safer with him than I ever was with the one whose touch was so terrifyingly desirable.

"Something wrong?" Reg asked, eying her closely.

"No. Why did you ask?"

"You looked . . . lost."

"What an odd thing for you to notice," she said softly.

"Not odd. I notice everything about you."

"You're an awfully nice person."

"Oh, sure. Good old Reg," he said with uncomfortable humor. "*Is* there something wrong?"

"We're getting a new roomer tomorrow. It always makes me feel funny."

"Don't know why the heck I can't take the room," he grumbled.

"Pop wouldn't think it was . . . suitable." A faint flush marked her cheeks, but, incredibly, Reg didn't seem to notice. They'd had this discussion before, and Reg refused to see it was not an acceptable plan. And, of course, it was, except that the neighbors wouldn't think so. If Reg were here, Pop would never need to have a moment's worry, she thought. Not about his leaving without notice, nor being overdue on his rent, nor oversolicitous with his daughters. But she was glad Reg didn't have the room. Even if he didn't care, she wanted some element of strangeness left in their relationship, some vestige of uncertainty.

"What'd you draw this time?" he asked.

"A college student. Wants to write his thesis in peace and says he can't do it in the fraternity house."

Reg frowned. "*His* thesis. I don't like the idea of college guys living here."

"Neither do I. Pop rented the room, we didn't."

"Well, stay away from him, that's all."

Rosemary stiffened. "Don't give me orders, Reg. I know what I'm doing, and how to behave (how well I know, she thought) but I won't be *told*."

"Sorry, kiddo. Didn't mean to step on your toes, or anything. It's just that . . . well, these college joes, some of them get ideas pretty fast."

"They get ideas if they're given them." Listen to me, she thought. Just do listen to me.

"Yeah, yeah, that's right," he said, looking at her as though she'd made a remarkably bright observation. "You and Lenore will know how to handle him."

"He'll probably be some inoffensive little grind who wouldn't notice us if we were served with parsley."

"Fat chance," Reg said gallantly.

"Who'll be?" Lenore asked, coming in. She picked up

a sweater and pulled it on. "It's cold in here, after the kitchen. I wish spring would come. You aren't going to serve me to anybody with parsley. Hank wouldn't like it." She drew her knitting box close and began to work expertly on a Hank-size pullover.

"We were talking about the new roomer," Rosemary said.

"Oh, him. Well, it really doesn't matter what he's like, does it? He's paid up the full month, incidentally. I think that's what won Pop over." Dropping her work to her lap, she said, "Rosie, am I wrong, or does he seem to be worrying more than usual about money?"

"Worried, I guess. But not more than usual. What else have we ever done, except worry?" She stopped, glanced irritably at Reg. That was the trouble, you got so used to having him around, almost like one of the family, that you spoke without thinking. I will not discuss our family situation, even with Reg, she told herself angrily. But he, with unusual tact, was saying to Lenore that he'd appreciate a sweater like that one very much, if she ever felt Hank had enough.

"Okay," Lenore grinned. "Next one for you, sweetie."

"You said we were going to celebrate," Rosemary reminded him. "What did you have in mind?"

Reg sat up. "Tell you what. I thought I'd go out later and get some pizza and beer, and we can look at the fights. How's that sound?"

"Just dandy," Rosemary said in a cold tone, and of course Reg was perfectly satisfied. It wasn't so much his not wanting to go out that stung her, since he *had* been driving almost steadily for three days. It was his bland assumption that pizza and the fights on television were a suitable celebration for what was, in his mind anyway, the halfway mark toward their marriage.

We might as well, she thought, be halfway through our married lives already, the way Reg acts. She looked at him, lazily smoothing his chin, eyes half closed, long legs sprawling, and felt that she could see him twenty years hence. The only difference, she decided, getting to her feet with a little snort of annoyance, is that he'll probably have colored television then, so he can *see* the blood and black eyes.

"Whatsa matter, honey?" he asked, yawning again.

"Matter? *Matter?* Why what could possibly be the matter? Haven't I everything a girl could ask? Beautiful warm home, elegant clothes, companionship. Who could be so selfish as to—"

Reg sat up. "What is it, Rosemary? Something I've done?" He looked at her a moment and added ruefully, "Or something I haven't?"

"Oh, Reg, no," she said, suddenly ashamed. "No. It's just that I . . . I get restless. Nothing ever seems to *happen.*"

"Well, gosh," he said in bewilderment, "you can't expect things to happen all the time. You'd be a nervous wreck. Anyway, don't you call getting up to two thousand bucks a thing that's happened?"

"Sure I do, Reg. Don't you see, though . . . Oh, no, I guess you don't. I guess you couldn't."

70

"Tell you what, Rosie. You're too jumpy. It's not good for a young girl to be so jumpy."

"Exactly what do you mean by that?" she inquired narrowly. Lenore, gathering her knitting, said she guessed she'd take a bath, and left the room. Neither Reg nor Rosemary seemed to notice.

"I asked you something," Rosemary said.

"Now, see here, Rosie, don't think you can fool me. You're spoiling for a little excitement, and if you can't have it any other way, you always pick a fight with me. Well, I'm not playing tonight. I'm tired, and I want to *look* at fights, not go a few rounds with you." He got up and put his arms around her. "Please, baby, let's . . . let's talk about what ails you, if you think it'd help, but no more of these phony battles you stir up. I tell you, it even interferes with my driving."

Held close, in the knowledge of love and protection, Rosemary subsided. "How does it?" she murmured, admitting to herself a certain pleasure that her power over Reg was so strong.

"I get worried and tired, that's how," he said huskily. "I get to thinking about it, and if we haven't made up, it's—" He groped for an explanation. "It's like when you aren't sure your dolly wheel is okay, see? You can drive all right, but the thing's on your mind, and you can't rest till you get it attended to. What are you shaking about?"

"I'm . . . I'm *laughing*," she burst out uncontrollably.

There was no further discussion about Rosemary's restlessness, and after a while the four of them, Hank and Lenore, Rosemary and Reg, ate pizza in the kitchen while Reg told them precisely why the dumb sausage had lost the decision. "Guy's got a right like a paddle coming up outa the water. I could change a tire and still catch him before he connected."

When, at about ten o'clock, Mr. Reed came in, he found the young people in the living room, drinking Cokes and beer, staring at the television screen, upon which a great many dashing events were being shared in by a great many glamorous people.

He paused uncertainly at the foot of the stairs, and then Reg turned and shouted, "Hi, Pop. Come on in and join the fun."

Smiling a little, Mr. Reed joined them. He was a staunch supporter of Reg Erskine, who was one fellow who could be relied on never to let his wife's relatives go without. And he wasn't in a hurry to get married, either, like some of these young devils. Patient and slow, that was Reg. Couple of years more of Rosemary's salary to help out, and then, if need be, a bit of a hand from Reg. Things looked pretty good to Mr. Reed, even if he did find it smarter to let the girls worry a little. "You bring them up," he often told his cronies over a glass of beer, "and then like as not they get married right out of high school and never give you another thought. It ain't right." Well, it wasn't going to be like that with James Reed, who missed his wife more than he realized, and did not realize at all that he might miss more than his daughters' help if they should leave him.

"What's happened up till now?" he asked, sitting down to study the television screen, and Lenore began

72

to explain in a low voice just what the beautiful people were up to.

"I don't know what he can be thinking of," Lenore mumbled sleepily, turning over in bed, "to move in on Saturday. Doesn't he know some people might be able to sleep? Your first Saturday off in weeks, and he has to move in. Doesn't he consider that people might have had a hard night watching television and would need their rest? Doesn't he—" She propped herself up on one elbow and stared at her sister.

Rosemary scrunched harder into her pillows, trying to pretend she was still asleep. The room was cold, and one of them would have to get up and close the window. If she waited long enough, and was quiet enough, maybe Lenore would just give in. Besides, she'd closed it yesterday, and the day before that. "Oh, I wish it were summer," she burst out, and so disclosed her wakefulness.

"I knew you were, anyway," Lenore said. She sprang across the room, pulled the window down, and was back in bed in seconds. She pulled the covers high and shuddered. "Almost worth it, don't you think? I mean, to get back in bed?"

"No, I don't." Rosemary stared at the ceiling, at a group of flower prints that she and Lenore had cut out of a magazine and framed, at the frost-bearded window. "Remember that man we had, Mr. Gibbons, who helped Pop with the furnace?"

"And got breakfast, too, once in a while."

"He was nice."

They sighed, expecting no such niceness from today's arrival. It would have been wonderful to keep Mr. Gibbons, but he had had to move on. It would be nice to get another such boarder, quiet, helpful, jolly in a subdued way. But no. It had to be a college boy, who would either be fresh or haughty (possibly both), who would not conceivably think to offer help with the furnace, and who would complain about the breakfasts, no matter what you gave him.

"And besides," Rosemary said now, sitting up and pulling toward her the clothes she'd laid on a bedside chair, "I don't believe that business about too much noise in the fraternity house."

"Don't believe it?"

"Well, think it over, Lenore. Why should this fellow not be able to study in a fraternity house when all the others can perfectly well? There's something phony about it, I tell you."

"Maybe," Lenore said slowly, "he's broke, and can't afford the house any more. Maybe he's saving his pride."

"For a month? Where's the sense in that? Do you think he's a remittance man and the last check got lost in Waterloo Station?"

"Maybe he's done something horrible and is being expelled for a month. A punishment for him."

"He'll find it a punishment, all right, living here after being in one of those places."

Those places were the dignified old private houses, large ones that had seen their day of huge families and were now, in the time of small houses and small families, serving as homes for well-off college students. The fraternities and sororities, set well back on their green lawns, on the beautifully treed streets of the finer parts of town. The high school lay beyond them, and for years Rosemary and Lenore had walked past these symbols of what they wanted and could not have. Truer symbols than the college buildings themselves, the mellowed, cut-fieldstone halls of knowledge that lay about the village square and were, to the people of Newellton, the heart of the town. To these two girls, and to others like them, the large old houses that sometimes blazed at night with light and music, that sometimes brooded, lit for study, that admitted warmly those who could enter and blandly denied the existence of those who could not, were the college.

Why, therefore, Rosemary asked herself, going downstairs in the still, cold house, would anyone want to leave, even for a month, a place like that to come to a place like this?

She found her father in the kitchen. He was making coffee, and he looked weary. Mr. Reed opened his candy store seven days a week, and had never, to their recollection, taken a vacation. Neither, for that matter, had they. It came to Rosemary with a sense of astonishment now and then that, except for brief visits to Boston, neither she nor Lenore had ever been anywhere, that neither of them had ever spent a night outside of this town. Once in a while, when she'd been in high school, Rosemary had visited overnight with a friend, and Lenore still did on occasion, but otherwise they were as much a part of their father's home as the roof above it.

She exchanged with him a silent good-morning nod, because he never did like to be spoken to before his coffee, and set about making oatmeal. The kitchen was much warmer than the rest of the house, and it was pleasant smelling the rough bubbling cereal, the sharp odor of coffee, the soft breath of the furnace's heat making its way up the stairs. How nice if it could always be like this, Rosemary thought. How nice not to have boarders, ever, but just the three of us—she looked up as Lenore came in and hugged her arms with pleasure at the warmth—just the three of us, like this. Not frantically happy, maybe, and certainly too poor, but alone.

Mr. Reed finished his second cup of coffee, accepted cereal, and said, shaking his head, "I dunno. Maybe I shouldn't of done it."

"Done what, Pop?" Though they all knew what he meant.

"Let this kid come here. We've never had boys before."

They hadn't. It had always been women, or girls, or men like Mr. Gibbons, who'd been a math teacher. It had been college girls without much money, college or high school teachers with small salaries and no families. But never a boy, and certainly never one who came from a fraternity house and paid a month in advance.

"The thing is," Mr. Reed went on, almost defiantly, "I got worried, not hearing from anybody. And you've got to admit no one else called before, or since." They nodded. "So—" he spread his hands "—what could I do?"

"Look, Pop," Lenore said, leaning across the table and patting his hand, "stop stewing, will you? It's only for a month, and if you're worried about Rosemary and me, well, don't. We know what we're doing."

"I know, I know." His puzzled eyes inspired them with unaccustomed affection. "Now, if your mother were still alive—" He blew out a futile breath.

Rosemary jumped to her feet. "We're all making too much of this," she told them. "It's a perfectly simple business transaction, and it will only be a month, so let's stop acting like we're about to set up house in a cemetery. When's he coming? What time? Did he say, Pop?"

" 'Bout two, he said. Gonna have lunch at his house and then drive over."

"Lunch?" Rosemary said suspiciously. "Where's he plan to eat his dinner?" She looked closely at her father, who avoided her eyes. "You *did* tell him that only breakfast goes with the room?"

"Well, now, that's the thing, Rosie," her father began, and both girls studied him sharply. He flapped an impatient hand, as though he could dispose of some troublesome thing that way, and then let it fall. "It's this way. This theme he's writing is going to take a lot of time, and he'd rather not have to bother driving over to his house to eat. The atmosphere, you see, might be distracting." He looked from one to the other of his daughters, encountered no help, and plodded on. "So

77

he'd rather eat all his meals here. Except lunch, that is," he added in an ameliorating tone. "Lunch he'll eat out."

"Dinner he'll eat out, too," Rosemary said.

"Nope. Dinner he eats here. He's already paid. Paid very handsomely, I might add."

"How handsomely do we have to feed him?" Lenore asked. But her voice accepted the fact that they would, indeed, cook dinner as well as breakfast for this bothersome new boarder. Rosemary, looking at her, accepted it, too.

"He said he didn't want things to be one bit different than what we always eat. He said he'd feel terrible if we changed anything at all for his sake. Just the way you folks eat, sir, that's what I want, he said."

Rosemary and Lenore exchanged a glance that encompassed prepared puddings, the cheaper cuts of meat, prunes and Spanish rice, stews stretched out with vegetables and dumplings. The things that they always ate.

"Well, that's dandy," Rosemary said. "If that's what he wants, I'm sure we'll be able to—accommodate him." She smiled at her father, who looked innocently back and said he was glad they were taking it that way.

After he'd gone, Rosemary and Lenore began to laugh.

"Canned hamburgers every other night," Lenore said, "with lots and lots of catsup, and mountains of bread, and rice pudding for dessert at least three times a week. Without raisins."

"One strip of bacon for breakfast Sunday mornings. And we'll go without. Just one strip, like a merit badge, on his plate."

"Just the way you folks eat, sir. That's what I want."

"Poor Pop," Lenore said.

"You know what I think? I think Pop is one of those people who's so afraid of being poor that he just can't help grabbing any money he can get."

"But he is poor. How can you be afraid of being something you already are?"

"I think it's the easiest thing in the world," Rosemary said sadly. "I mean, look at me. I'm scatter-brained and restless, and I'm certainly afraid of being like that."

"You aren't scatter-brained. And being restless is all right, I guess. Under the right circumstances."

"But who's to say which are the right ones?"

"Well . . . yourself, I suppose."

That's what gets me afraid, Rosemary thought. I just don't know. But she smiled at her sister and suggested that now was as good a time as any to get at the housecleaning. "We can have it done before he gets here if we hurry."

Their housecleaning was so routinized through long practice—Rosemary doing all that required washing, like the kitchen, bathrooms, woodwork, and Lenore managing the vacuum, duster, and linen changing— that they had time to compose themselves in the living room, each with a book, before a car drew up to the house and the new boarder got out.

The car was a Plymouth, and not too new, but that told them nothing. They'd learned from Reg about what he called the "small car snobs." Reg's boss, who owned a fleet of fifty trucks, wouldn't be caught dead in any car bigger than a Buick. "Lots of them are that way," Reg had said. "They think it's ostentatious to enjoy their money." Reg loved big, quiet, expensive cars, and if he ever had any money, it was safe to say he would not be a small car snob. Still, the Plymouth told them nothing. The clothes did. As the young man got his luggage from the rear seat, they had a chance to observe what was unquestionably a cashmere coat.

"How can you be sure?" Lenore asked, as they crowded each other at the window, safely concealed behind imitation lace curtains.

"Darling, after all my years in that store I should be able to recognize cashmere. It's cashmere."

The luggage, two leather suitcases and a typewriter, spoke of travel and good origins. And the boy himself, when he turned and stood a moment looking curiously at the house before starting up the walk, told them without a word what they'd wondered about. He held himself in that self-assured, relaxed manner that only those born to self-assurance could communicate. It was a quality Jay Etting had. It did not make a person kind, nor generous, nor intelligent (though Rosemary supposed remotely it did not preclude those traits), but it made him at home anywhere. And it made Rosemary, who felt so terribly excluded and constrained in unfamiliar atmospheres, nervous and hostile before he'd so much as rung the bell.

They went together to meet him, Lenore first, Rosemary trailing and biting her lip and wondering how you could serve a dinner of Spanish rice and string beans to this person. She wished her father had told them exactly how handsomely the boarder had paid for his meals. Just what they had every night would probably come as a surprise to—she realized they didn't even know his name—him, and might make him feel they were cheating. Had he paid for meat every night, and butter instead of oleo? What *had* he paid for? Sometimes, she thought with a nervous shake of the head, as Lenore opened the door, sometimes Pop was just plain unreasonable in his refusal to talk to them about money. Look at the position he'd put them in now. Look at—

"I'm sorry," Lenore was saying, as she stepped back to allow him entry in the little hall, "that we don't know your name. But we're Rosemary and Lenore Reed. We're—" she tipped an eyebrow slightly "—your landladies."

The boy looked a bit startled. He dropped his luggage, looked from one to the other of the plainly dressed, pretty, faintly chilling girls who confronted him, and put out his hand. Lenore took it briefly. Rosemary merely nodded.

"I'm Sam Lyons." He had one of those very deep young men's voices. "It's good of you to have me," he added, and glanced down at his bags, as though, Rosemary thought, he expected room service to appear and take them.

"Not at all," she said. "After all, the room is for rent." Lenore gave her a stern glance, which she ignored. "If you'd like to take your things, I'll show it to you. The room."

She started up the stairs, and after a moment Mr. Lyons followed. When they arrived at the master bedroom, Rosemary discovered that Lenore had carried the typewriter, and for some reason that made her furious. "You'll find towels and things, everything you'll need. I guess." Everything you'll get, her voice implied. "And we understand you'll be eating with us?"

He nodded. "I'd hoped to. My thesis, you know—"

"Yes. Well, we eat dinner pretty early. Six o'clock." She started out of the room, turned, and added, "Mr. Lyons, you do understand that our food is—simple? That we haven't the time or the—the money (how much *had* he paid?) to prepare anything elaborate?"

"I explained to your father, Miss Reed, that I wanted just what you have. I really did mean it. Besides, food doesn't mean much to me, one way or the other."

"Well, then—" Rosemary hesitated, could think of nothing more to say, and was under the impression that she'd already said too much, too unpleasantly. But there was nothing to do about it. She left the room, heard Lenore's, "Well, anyway, here you are, and if you want anything, give us a call," and went downstairs, to the living room, where she picked up the book she had not been reading before and proceeded not to read it again.

Lenore came in and stood before her, arms folded, till Rosemary was forced to look up.

"Well, what's your trouble?" Rosemary asked.

"I meant to ask that of you. Do you realize how rude you've been?"

"Don't talk to me that way, Lenore. You go cozy up to him all you want, but I'm not going to."

"I was not cozying up to him, and you know it. I was being ordinarily courteous, and you behaved as if you'd been brought up in a barn." Rosemary flushed, but her sister went on. "If he'd been someone else—a girl, or a teacher or something—you'd have recalled your manners, but just because he's a college boy and you hate all college boys since Jay Etting—oh, yes, you do—I don't know how much that boy hurt you, and I hate him myself for whatever he did to you, but I'll hate him more if it ruins your own sense of self-respect to a point where you can be plain unmannerly and not even care," she finished breathlessly.

"I don't care how much you hate him," Rosemary said sullenly, knowing her sister was right, ashamed of herself and unable to admit it.

"What I feel about *him* has nothing to do with it—"

"You're the one who brought it up."

For a long moment they looked at each other, Rosemary with her head tipped up a little, Lenore standing over her like a disapproving parent. Then Lenore turned and left the room. Rosemary, staring at the floor, her skin damp and chilly, thought, I wish I were dead. The words did not seem melodramatic, simply a statement of fact. She wished she were through with this life that she seemed to be making, more and more, all the time, a hopeless, graceless muddle. She thought of Reg, who loved her in spite of her follies, her inconsistencies, her rudeness. Only, she reminded herself, getting up, this was the first time she'd ever been deliberately rude. Sam Lyons was not responsible for Jay Etting, and in any case he was a guest, paying, to be sure, but a guest under their roof.

She went into the kitchen and found Lenore studying the pantry shelves with a worried frown.

"Lenore, I'm sorry."

Her sister turned. "Oh gosh, Rosemary, I knew you wouldn't really be rude. I mean, not for long." She looked searchingly at Rosemary. "Is there anything about that Etting character? I mean, anything it would help you to talk about—"

"No," Rosemary said quickly. "I don't want to talk about him ever, not at all."

"I see." Once again they stared at each other in bafflement, and then Lenore said, "I was thinking we could have Welsh rarebit and stewed tomatoes. I could make biscuits."

"Doesn't seem like very much, does it?"

"It's what we would have had. One of us could make a pie, I suppose. Are there any canned cherries? Yes, there are. You want to make the pie and I'll do the other stuff?"

"Might as well."

They gathered their materials and shortly were working in the rhythmic, easy way they had, companionable in the warm kitchen. Outside, the waning afternoon was cold and hard, and the intermittent traffic had a discontented whining sound. In the summer, Rosemary thought, as she dreamily rolled the pie crust, all sounds are softened, gentled somehow. But at this time of year everything clanks and creaks. Chains on snow, tree branches in the wind, icicles snapping free of the eaves. The only softness of winter is the snow, and how quickly that becomes hard, or slushily treacherous. And how thin everything is in the winter air, how thin your blood becomes, and your voice, and even your thoughts and feelings. Stiff and thin. There isn't any richness about winter, she thought. It's a skinny, huddled season, like a bad-tempered animal that wants to bite and is only waiting for a chance.

"You know," she said, "I really like the kitchen better than any other room in the house."

"I do, this time of year," Lenore agreed. She opened a can of tomatoes. "If I put cubes of bread in this, will it seem like too much? I mean, having biscuits under the rarebit too?"

"It's what we'd usually do," Rosemary quoted her sister.

"He's awfully quiet, isn't he?" Lenore said. When Rosemary did not reply, she went on, "I feel sort of sorry for him, in a way. His room won't be awfully warm, you know, and it must be sort of strange—a different house and all, and no one talking to him."

"He's not the type to feel strange anywhere."

"How do you know?"

"I just do."

"Maybe. I still think it might be nice to *ask* if he'd like to sit in the kitchen for a while."

"Do as you please."

Naturally, Lenore did not invite him.

At dinner, Mr. Reed was cumbersomely sociable. He called Sam Lyons "young fellow" and made several humorous comparisons between the place he'd left and the place in which he now found himself.

"Which one of the frat houses did you say you came from?" he inquired.

Rosemary and Lenore winced at the "frat," but Sam Lyons said readily, "I'm a Deke, sir."

"A Deke, now. That'd be the big stucco place on the corner of Willow and Third. A very handsome house, all right, very, *very* handsome. Used to belong to the Ameses. A very important family hereabouts, the Ameses were. Of course that was before your time. About 1890," he added ingenuously. "Then there was some family, the Regans, took over for a while. Nothing much but money to recommend *them*. And they lost it, after a bit, ran clean through it. Fools and their money, you know. Takes a bit of cash to run that place proper. Now, let's see, haven't I seen you in my little shop? Plenty of these Deke boys come in, to hang around like, drinking Cokes. Sort of like a club to them, I suppose."

I won't be able to stand this, Rosemary thought. She looked pleadingly at her father, who was, however, so occupied with letting the new boarder know he had come to the right sort of home, the sort that comprehended college men and their ways, that he missed her desperate signal.

"Seems to me like I might have seen you in my little shop," Mr. Reed repeated.

"Well . . . generally I stick sort of close to the house,"
Sam Lyons said. "Don't get to this end of town much."

Much, thought Rosemary.

"Sort of a lone wolf, eh?" said Mr. Reed. "I was sorta
like that myself, as a young fellow. Take people or
leave 'em alone, that's how I was. Still am, for the matter
of that."

Oh, Pop, Pop, Rosemary mourned. She looked at
Lenore, who lifted her shoulders a little and then applied
herself to Welsh rarebit.

"Mr. Lyons," Rosemary said loudly, "I understand you
found things too noisy at your fraternity house. I just
wanted to tell you that here you'll be quite undisturbed."

Sam Lyons looked from Rosemary to Lenore, and
unexpectedly grinned. "I'm beginning to gather that,"
he said. "In fact, I can truthfully say that I've never been
so completely undisturbed in my life as I was this afternoon."

"That's fine, that's fine," said Mr. Reed. "These girls
of mine understand about studying. A pair of students,
the both of them. In fact, it's a downright shame they
didn't get to go on to college. I wanted them to, mind,
but—"

At this, even Lenore boggled. She jumped to her feet
and said, "How about pie, Mr. Lyons? Pop, do have a
piece of pie, because if you don't hurry, you'll be late
back to the store. And you certainly don't want to be
late back to the—" She broke off, ran a flustered hand
across her brow, and began to clear the dishes noisily.

Rosemary got up to help, and between them they

talked enough and rattled dishware and silver enough to quiet even a determined Mr. Reed. Rosemary glanced once at Sam Lyons, who was quietly studying them, his eyes going from one to the other, with what appeared to be a good deal of interest. He was a slender, nice-looking young man, dark of hair, blue-eyed, with a mobile, faintly humorous expression. But the humor, Rosemary thought, is being plentifully supplied. Who the heck wouldn't be amused at the show we're putting on? Pop spouting like a silly fish, Lenore and me shouting at the tops of our voices and practically throwing the china around?

She put a piece of pie in front of him, poured his coffee, asked if he took sugar and cream, and all the while she was telling him silently, "You are an interloper, Mr. Lyons. And, Mr. Lyons, I do not like you."

CHAPTER FIVE

ON SATURDAY MORNING, HELENA WILLIAMS ROLLED OVER in bed, eyed her creamed, curlered, sleeping roommate with a frown, listened to the hivelike depth of her breathing, and whispered, "Roxanne! Roxanne, turn over, *please.*"

Roxanne sighed, and did not wake, and slowly turned over. For a while there was quiet in the room, except for the cheerful ticking of the clock that in less than an hour would remind Helena of History II, her only Saturday class, one which began at eight o'clock. Dr. Hawkins would be there before any of his class arrived, arranging his papers with chirpy good humor, glancing up with a genuine smile as his students assembled, beginning his lecture with a brisk assumption that everyone was eager and prepared to discuss *The Federalist Papers* at slightly past eight in the morning.

Helena smiled a little, decided to get what sleep there was remaining, punched her pillow, pulled her night-dress down, the covers up, closed her eyes, opened them again, decided it was impossible. She flung herself around as Roxanne's gentle buzzing resumed. Oh well, so be it. In half an hour it wouldn't matter. In an hour she'd be trudging across the cold campus to Merton Hall and Dr. Hawkins and Alexander Hamilton. She looked at the window, at the frost webs in the corners of the panes, and fell asleep.

When the alarm chattered into her dreams like a startled animal, she sat upright, blinking and disheveled. Why, she wondered, hushing the frantic bell, does the last sleep come so deeply, the one just before waking? As if you were losing something—which you were—and would never regain it—which you would.

She moved about the room, rubbing her arms, trying to be quiet as she collected robe and soap and towel. Yawning, she went down the hall to the bathroom.

"Hi, Helena," said a girl at the washstand, her lips frothy with toothpaste.

"Hi, Anne."

Anne McGinnis rinsed her mouth, peered at her reflection in the mirror, turned away. " 'Bye," she murmured.

" 'Bye."

It was as much of a salutation as anyone could contrive at that hour.

But when, dressed and brushed and hungry, they encountered each other at the dining-room door, it was as if they'd been awake for hours. There was, Helena reflected over orange juice, a certain pre-eminence in being one of those who woke and worked while others lay abed. She said this to Anne.

"I suppose so," Anne admitted, "once you're up. But

it's the perishing getting-up part. Almost takes away the pre-eminence, if you see what I mean."

"Oh, clearly. But it doesn't for me. In fact, I sort of like not wanting to get out of bed. Makes everything even more so later on. If you see what I mean."

"Dimly. Smacks of masochism." She looked around at the few other diners, and back to Helena. "There is something to it, I guess."

"Well, now, take Roxanne. She'll wake up in a rumpled bed at something like eleven o'clock, and the best part of the day will be gone, and she'll be starving and have to go to a drugstore, or wait till lunch—" She broke off, mention of the drugstore having recalled Rosemary Reed. "Do you ever get over to that drugstore on Chauncey Street and—and Oak, I guess it is?"

"What in the world for? No, I don't suppose I have. I don't get to Chauncey Street much."

"It's not so far," Helena said absently. "Jay and I walked over there, about a week ago. The night it snowed so."

"You and Jay seeing each other again?"

Helena looked up, a little surprised. Jay's name had been so incidental to her thoughts about Rosemary that she had scarcely noticed saying it. "No. Not really. He just wanted to talk, or something. Look, Anne, tell me what you think about this town versus college people business."

"At this hour?" Anne began lightly, and then, at Helena's expression, said, "I disapprove."

"Yes, and I bet you wouldn't find anyone in the college who wouldn't answer that way. But—it still obtains, doesn't it? The division, the drawing apart? Here's the college, there's the town, and when are the twain going to meet?"

"They meet. Town people come to our games and all. And once in a while one of the town girls gets invited—"

"That's what I'm trying to say, don't you see? The minute you remember that it was my—practically my steady—who asked a town girl to a college dance, you go all flustered and can't continue."

"Only because it *was* your steady. And if you don't mind my saying so, you certainly seemed to take it hard."

"I don't mind. I didn't really, but I'll never get anyone to believe me. But the fact still remains that if one of the fellows takes a town girl out, she's very apt to get the freeze treatment, in spite of all we say about disapproving."

"I haven't seen it happen often enough to judge. That girl, of course—"

"That girl what?" Helena prompted.

Anne lifted her shoulders. "She was— She had a heart too easily made glad. Liked whate'er she looked on and her looks went everywhere. You know the kind. Why, she even embarrassed some of the boys."

"Why, I wonder?"

"Some boys do get embarr—"

"No, why she acts that way. Used to do it in high school, too. Only then she got away with it. I never stopped to wonder if there was some reason . . . Well, I didn't used to wonder." Not, she thought, until the night she'd seen the slender, insufficiently clothed,

92

rather awkward Rosemary in the drugstore, who had so little fitted her picture of the Rosemary she knew in high school.

"You wouldn't have wondered if you'd been there," Anne said, and Helena was unreasonably annoyed.

"It is," she said, reverting, "a very real factor in this town, and I think it's funny the way we study and spout about democracy all the time in class, and then think it's perfectly all right to say 'town people,' as if they were a different species. An inferior one."

"Nothing much to do about it. Unless you want to start a crusade." Anne began to gather her books. "If you do, of course, I'd probably be willing to go along for the ride."

Helena shook her head. "No, I'm not the crusading type. And going along for the ride is not the crusading spirit."

"If I've read my history correctly, it was going along for the ride and the riches and nothing else. If a genuine crusader, in that—spiritual—sense of the word, got mixed up in it, he was probably unhorsed and robbed by his cohorts before he got well out of London."

"My gosh, everybody's cynical."

"Not cynical. Practical. It's an inelegant and cut-throat world, dear. Just as much now as then. Maybe more so."

"And don't you think that's sad?" Helena, too, collected her books, and they walked to the hall closet, where they drew on boots, heavy parkas, mittens of fleecy wool. "Don't you?" she insisted.

They went out the door, and turned toward Merton

Hall. The morning brimmed with sunlight and quiet cold. Where the plows had piled it to either side of the street, snow formed jagged walls of ice, and beneath their feet patches of ice had a dull mackerel-like iridescence. They shivered and walked quickly.

"Sure I think it's sad," Anne answered. "But it's what we have, and there's nothing either one of us can do about it. Nothing much anyone can do about it, I guess, when you look at the people who've tried. Patrick Henry, and Lincoln, and St. Francis and all. If they couldn't do anything about the way of the world and people, how can we? And the more they tried, the more of a mess things got to be, that's what I think."

"Maybe things would be worse if people like that hadn't done all they could."

"Maybe. And if you're made like them, you have to try in spite of yourself. But I don't see *how* things could be much worse. The world's full of bigots and tyrants and bombs."

"Full of people trying to cure bigotry and convert tyrants and turn bombs into power plants."

"So it is. You know, Helena, I bet you'll be one of the ones who goes in a cellar when the bombs fall and then comes out and tries to rebuild on the rubble."

"And you?"

"Oh, I'll just sit and get hit. I don't want to rebuild civilization. If the world as I know it, pitiful as it is, is going to be blown up, then I want to be blown up with it."

"I'm not sure you're right about me. But somebody has to be willing to rebuild."

94

"Why?" said Anne.

They arrived at Merton Hall with no answer from Helena. And they didn't think to ask such questions of Mr. Hawkins, whose interest in wars ended with Appomattox.

After class, Helena went to the library and withdrew two books on English usage. She was not sure yet how to go about the paper she and Roxanne had thought of, but the notion of presenting Mr. Warner with two papers written independently but intentionally on the same topic was appealing. It would, she knew, appeal to Mr. Warner, who loved words better than—better than anything, it seemed to his students. He taught literature, but it occurred to everyone who studied with him that his interest was far less in what was being said than in which words the writer said it. He visibly winced at misused words. People who inferred when they should have implied; who praised fulsomely when they meant to be sincere. "Fulsome praise, indeed," he'd mutter. "And half the people so praised don't even know enough to be insulted." Mr. Warner's favorite writers were Pope and Fowler, and he valued above rubies the student who never said "the reason is because," and never used like as a conjunction. A little, rather desiccated man, who was fun to work for, if you liked words, too, and Helena did.

She paused at the desk for a few words with Mrs. Powell, then walked back to the house, musing now upon her evening's date with Jay. She'd made up her mind what to do and did not find it pleasant. Still, with

Jay only the strongest measures would work, the most obvious devices. Telling him a thing was useless, subtlety was lost upon him, so there remained only unkindness, or, to put it more bluntly, rudeness. He's brought it on himself, she thought defensively. If he'd let me alone, this wouldn't have had to happen. But she wished it didn't have to happen, and she wished she'd feel more comfortable about it.

"I got these two books," she told Roxanne, who was sitting, tousle-haired and heavy-lidded, on the edge of her bed.

"Mmm." Roxanne wiggled her toes, yawned, and said, "What two books?"

"These. For our papers."

"What papers?"

"Skip it. I'll start over again when you wake up."

Roxanne nodded, yawned again, got up, and wandered to her closet muttering about the sickening alertness of people who liked to get up in the morning.

"I suppose I could talk about the sickening inertness of people who don't," Helena said, but by then Roxanne had disappeared toward the showers. Helena, making her bed, dusting the furniture, sorting her books, reverted to the conversation she and Anne had had earlier. Like so many conversations, it had started out one way, got sidetracked almost immediately, and never returned to the starting point. What did Anne think about town people versus college people, as terms, and as human beings? Anne didn't approve of classifying people one way or the other, and practically no one approved. And everyone went right on doing it. She remembered the minister saying once that Christ was crucified because the greater populace, though vaguely sympathetic toward Him, was yet too self-interested, too indifferent, to raise a cry in His defense. And that's the way it's been ever since, she thought. We disapprove of injustice and inhumanity and think our disapproval makes us just and humane. Then we forget all about it, and the next time make our contribution of indifference, and so the cross continues to be occupied. The extravagance of her own thoughts made her a bit self-conscious, yet she would not deny them. Because that's what it was, truly, even with its air of melodrama. Indifference, injustice, were a form of crucifixion.

Yet the more you examined what was so clearly a truth, the clearer it became that Anne was right, there was nothing to do about it. The difference between the town people and the college people was not a difference that lay in superiority or inferiority. It was a difference of interests. Helena considered that and found a degree of comfort. Not injustice, not indifference, after all, but simple divergence of paths. And divergence, diversity, was surely something no one would want changed? Thinking she had settled something for herself, she turned from the subject with relief.

When Roxanne returned, Helena was ready to leave.

"Where are you off to now?" Roxanne demanded. "Bounding in and out this way like a kangaroo. You just got here, and it's practically lunchtime. Thank heaven."

"Look, Roxanne, I'm going home. But the thing is—"

Roxanne looked suspicious. "I don't care for sentences that begin, the thing is—"

"Who does? The thing is this—I'm going home, but if anyone calls, you don't know where I am. Do you understand?"

"Not at all."

"Well, it doesn't matter if you do or don't. Just if you're asked, I left this morning and won't be back till tomorrow night. Period."

Roxanne looked as if she might be going to inquire further, then apparently found her appetite greater than her curiosity. "I'm going down to eat. Best to your folks," was all she said.

It was peculiar, Helena found it most peculiar, how every now and then when she left one place for another, she left with a sense of escape. No matter whether it was home or school, she departed with a delightful feeling of release. She wondered if other people often felt this way. Perhaps it was not very becoming in her, perhaps it showed a vein of restlessness or even dissatisfaction, but she liked it. Now, moving swiftly down the street toward the bus stop, she realized that the sensation of freedom and lightness came only when she was alone. If Roxanne had been with her, with plans to spend the night at the house, it would simply be a trip across town. But alone— oh, alone it could be a journey to the end of the world. I like to be alone, she thought. It seemed to her that pleasure in aloneness (not loneliness) must be one of the good gifts given at the cradle. How pitiful, how really ignoble, to be always in search of companionship, the way Jay was, and so many others she knew.

She boarded the bus, settled by a window, and continued to turn this conception over in her mind. To be alone was not the wish, it appeared, of most people in school, where cliques and couples and crowds abounded and only the misfits were solitary. Yet I, she thought, am not one of those. She gave a little sigh of pleasure. It had not always been so. In high school she had been, not precisely a misfit, but not, ever, one of the inner, select crowd. Aloneness then had so often been not through choice. Rosemary, now . . . she had been so popular, so always the center of a crowd, and even if there'd been talk about *how* she achieved her eminence, that was not much comfort to girls who could not share it. And there were plenty of girls back then just as wild about boys as Rosemary had been, who only managed to be laughed at or talked about aloud. The speculation about Rosemary had been muted. Present, but rarely put into words. She . . . Well, Helena decided helplessly, Rosemary had had that quality known as "an air." Rosemary had had a way about her and she'd cut a wide swathe through high school. Helena, an only child of prosperous parents, had had as much to offer in the way of looks, and more in the way of opportunities to dress dashingly and entertain. But she hadn't known how to offer what she had.

I always wanted to have parties at home when I was in high school, she thought, and I never gave but that one.

Her mother and father had wanted her to have

parties, too. "Darling," Mrs. Williams would say, "why don't you invite your gang over after the football game? I'll have sandwiches and cake and hot chocolate, and your father and I will stay upstairs. You can roll back the rugs and—"

But Helena would shake her head. "It's already made up that we're to go to Esther's." Or Phyllis', or Rosemary's, or, once in a while, one of the boys' homes, though the parents of boys rarely seemed to think of parties in connection with their own homes. Having produced a boy was apparently contribution enough in their eyes. (Certainly the girls gave them every reason to think so.) And Helena got invited to all the parties. Not a wallflower, not a misfit. I could go to them and be accepted, she thought, but I could not draw them to me.

And then she had fallen in love. The first love, the one that is lost but never, never relinquished. Harold Daniels, whom she had known since grade school, who had, when they were small, ridden her home on the handle bars of his bicycle, requested her as a partner in seventh grade dancing school, and forgotten her as she had him by the time they were each thirteen, had looked at her one day when they were juniors in high school, and smiled and said, "I traded my bike in on a flivver. Would you just as soon ride home in that?" And so the world and the endless love began as they bucked and squeaked toward her house in an indestructible Ford.

That had been in winter, and in the spring she said, "Mom, about that party—" Ignoring her mother's too bright smile, she went on, "Nothing elaborate. Just a sort of—spread. Saturday, maybe. Sometime when I can get them all together."

Two Saturdays later the house was lit and filled with music, and the gang, as she knew it, the ones who hung together forming this particular crowd, were dancing in the Williamses' beautiful living room. The rugs were rolled back, and there was a too elaborate but delectable buffet, and Helena's heart was broken.

Now, years—four years—later, it did not seem important. She could remember the terrible hurt, the terrible, necessary smile she wore, the crippling length of the evening as she watched Rosemary gaily, casually, waken a bright response and eagerness in Harold's eye. The boy Rosemary was with turned sulky, Helena grew desperately gracious, the speculative eyes moved over the four of them, and the more this potpourri of emotion and reaction was stirred, the more animated Rosemary became. She seemed to become prettier, more radiant. No one, Helena had thought, drugged with pain and the endlessness of the evening, could compete with her. She wins before she even begins. Stiff, aching, desperate with the need to be alone in her room, Helena had endured the evening, and, at last, trembling with the effort, said goodbye to the last guests. Her goodbye to Harold had been a triumph, had it not? A handshake, a quick smile, a turning to the next person, which dismissed him quite completely. No, it didn't seem important now . . . a thing she could remember, but need not relive. Only, at times, she felt that that evening, that suffering and the surprise at how deeply you could suffer without betraying it, were engraved somewhere in her life, still quivering and sentient. That evening was like a place once visited and left behind. You need never return to it, but now and then, without warning, the consciousness of its existence returns to you. Harold had called her once or twice after that, had stopped her in the hall with a puzzled expression and an offer of a ride home. She had smiled the meaningless smile and refused, and after a while he stopped all attentions. He had not, either, appeared to see much of Rosemary after the first few weeks following the party.

In other words, Helena thought now, getting up to leave the bus, it all came to nothing. And nothing was all it was. Just an experience, a very ordinary one, and finished. Where Harold was, she did not know. Rosemary, with so much of her sparkle lost that Helena could not even quite dislike her any more, was no part of Helena's life. And mine? she asked herself. My life is fine. I have friends, and people who like to come to my house, I know how to offer the things I have, and I like being alone. I'm not in love, but some day I shall be, and then I'll know how to fight for what I need. Meanwhile there was an intoxicating sense of freedom from love and its demands.

She walked down the street toward her home. Chilled now, after the warmth of the bus, but light-footed. Her mother, looking up as she came in the door, had the impression of something airborne.

"My, you look . . . complacent," she said with amusement. Since Helena had entered college, her mother's old enfolding protectiveness had given way to a pleased and pleasing friendliness. Everything, after all, had turned out well for this, their only child. There was no need to yearn over her any longer, no need to give her too many things to assuage her, and them, for the things she could not have. Mrs. Williams felt that they'd been blessed, and happily slipped into a role of loving but unanguished motherhood. "Very complacent," she said, looking at her daughter's glowing cheeks and eyes.

"Well, I am, I guess. Aren't you surprised to see me?"

"Sort of. Are you going to stay tonight?"

"Yup." Helena hung her coat in the hall closet, removed her boots, entered the living room, where her mother was sorting and entering checks in the book. "Having a hard time?"

"Not at all."

"You should be more feminine. It's not genteel for ladies to balance checkbooks easily, and I'm sure it's lacking in respect for Dad."

"He'll gladly suffer disrespect if only I'll take care of the checks." Mrs. Williams closed the book, slipped the remaining checks into an envelope, closed the top of the little desk she used, and turned to her daughter. "Why are you home?" she inquired. "Not that we don't love having you, but—"

"I have my reasons. Very good ones, but not to be divulged."

"Your father and I are going out to dinner tonight. Or, at least—" She paused uncertainly. "If we'd known you were going to be home, dear—"

"Mother, don't be a stupe. If I were home from UCLA, I might expect you to abandon all plans. But this way . . . how silly. And besides, all I want is a quiet evening at home. I won't even answer the telephone."

"Is there something wrong?" Mrs. Williams inquired, in a voice that proved the old protectiveness was there, should it be called upon.

"Nothing at all in the world. Didn't you get tired, once in a while, of girls and their voices and their plots and their undies hanging everywhere when you were in college?"

"Oh, yes. Of course I couldn't get home the way you can, so I just put up with it." Mrs. Williams smiled dreamily. "It was easy to put up with."

"Do you miss it?"

"Miss it? Why, darling, of course not. It would be sort of freakish to go around missing college when you get to be my age. It was nice to have had, something to remember. You'll find that out, when you get older. You'll look at your own daughter and think, Well, such a lot has changed, but a few constants are always with us. Like trigonometry, and popcorn, and undies on the towel racks."

"What's changed?"

Mrs. Williams looked baffled for a moment, and then said, "Clothes, of course. In my day we wore silk stockings, and dresses." Helena looked horrified. "Well, naturally you think no one but a buffoon would wear anything but Bermuda shorts and knee-length socks before dinner. But such things simply weren't known when

I was a girl. You girls dress much more sensibly," she added. "And it makes you so much—so much more appealing when you do dress up. Like phoenixes, rising from ashes of jeans and shirttails."

Helena smiled. "And what else has changed?"

"Well, I guess—far more than the change in clothes —there's been a change in what you might call atmosphere, attitude." Mrs. Williams paused, examined her wedding ring, and went on. "I was in school during a period when it was considered quite smart to dodge as much work as possible and to play, if anything, more than was possible. It was the age when people who studied seriously were known as 'grinds.' I don't think that exists much any more, does it?"

Helena shook her head slowly. "Very little. No, not much of that, I guess."

"Well, we seemed to divide up between the grinds and the butterflies. All work or all play. I played."

"Didn't you get good marks?"

"Sometimes. I never failed anything, but I do distinctly recall bragging about how close I'd come to failing." She shook her head. "But there's something more than that about you young people today. It's a seriousness, a sense of responsibility, I think. I notice that college people, and even high school people, seem to care a good deal more about how the world is going than we did. Where it's going. My friends and I made a point of not knowing or caring."

"You must have been in with a pretty lightweight group," Helena said a bit severely.

"Perhaps. There were a great many of us. Today's attitude is much finer. Better for the world. It almost gives me hope for it, to see how soberly the young people read and discuss things. To see how much they know. And then—there isn't the snobbery, the class consciousness—"

"Why, Mother, how can you say that? There's the most utter class consciousness right here in this town that you could ever run into. What else leads to terms like 'town people'? I agree that there doesn't seem to be as much race consciousness as there used to be, or if there is, at least it's out in the open and people are trying to do something about it. But class consciousness . . . I don't believe we've done a thing to change that."

"I never use the term myself. Town people," Mrs. Williams said. "The fact that it's used at the college is—just a term of differentiation, isn't it? The way you'd say one group is professional and one is business?"

"It isn't that simple, by a long shot," Helena said, and was silent for a few minutes. "I can't really explain it, though heaven knows I seem to think about it all the time lately. I'm beginning to bore the kids around the house."

"What have you done about it?"

"Well, but *nothing*. I can't think of anything to do. I don't like—inequities. I hated it that Phyllis Bookman was so hurt that time, and yet I couldn't get the girls at school mad at me, could I?"

"Why not?"

"Because I have to live with them, that's why not."

And because, she thought suddenly, I'm still not sure enough of myself to run risks. She jumped to her feet. "Have done, Mama. This is all too serious on an empty stomach."

"Darling," said Mrs. Williams, rising quickly. "Of course, you'll be wanting your lunch. Shall I tell Nona to serve us both in here, on trays?"

That phrase lip service, Helena thought, certainly covers much and applies often. And yet she relaxed, as after the rigors of an examination. Too much thinking, too much of it frustrated, on the one subject had wearied and confused her. After a while it was better to put the thoughts away and turn to the little, minute-occupying matters. Lunch. What to do this afternoon. More important, how tonight would be.

That was a problem, indeed . . . tonight and how it would go.

Jay arrived at the library, a small florist's box tucked under his arm, at slightly before eight o'clock in the evening. Why she wanted to meet him here rather than have him call at the house was anybody's guess, but he'd do, at the moment, most things within reason to conciliate her. Most things, he repeated to himself, and felt a flicker of resentment that was hard to snuff out. Never, not since he'd first noticed girls—and that was lord knew how many years ago—never had one turned on him the way Helena was doing. She acted through jealousy, that was plain enough, but her *firmness* . . . it was baffling and annoying and, he insisted to himself, intriguing. Jay was too much of a performer not to recognize the emotions appropriate to such a stereotyped situation, too much of a conformist not to act upon them. And, he thought, putting the thick shiny box beside him on a bench, it *was* sort of intriguing, if she didn't carry it too far. He thought he could rely on Helena to know when to draw a line.

The library was doing a good evening business. Brightly lighted, softly murmurous, a good deal of muted activity in the stacks, the tables well occupied with severely serious students. Funny how the atmosphere of the place could make the veriest clowns look scholarly. There was old Bub Holden, heaviest quarterback on the East Coast, burrowing into three books at once, scribbling furiously, biting his lip with concentration. Things *are* stereotypes, Jay decided. Reasonably, Bub should turn out to be a good student, an applied and earnest one, or else he'd be like a quarterback in the movies. Still, he was like a quarterback in the movies, panting after the minimum grades, the coach breathing hotly down his neck. At another table was the blonde he'd seen at Helena's house. Pretty thing, all down and cashmere, writing with a little silver pencil. He frowned a bit, and shifted his position so as to be out of her purview. Fine thing if it got around that he was kept waiting—he glanced up at the clock to check—kept waiting in the library while Helena took her sweet time. Again that slight rise of temper that must be subdued.

Sitting back, hands in his lap, he relaxed consciously. Helena was a capricious and unpredictable girl, but she was the one he wanted most of all. The gayest, almost the prettiest, certainly the most disturbing (for which, he thought, read exciting) he'd ever met, and he'd been ten kinds of a fool to get tangled up with Rosemary Reed—*that* one—when he'd known for sure how Helena would react. Not that he'd wanted for a minute to take the Reed girl to the dance that night, but a guy would have had to be made of stone to disappoint the poor thing, all dressed up by mistake. Had it been by mistake? Jay was inclined now to think he'd been duped. Duped? Why—he took a deep breath and admitted it to himself—he'd been given a plain runaround. Tricking him into the dance to begin with, then making a fool of herself over everyone from Bub on down, then pulling the freeze when he tried to— He scratched his chin, shifted again, crossed his legs. Well, it happened to the best of people. A teaser was a teaser and he'd like to know anyone who hadn't run into one sometime. He wasn't precisely easy in his mind about the way he'd sort of let the fellows think she'd been less of a teaser and more of a performer than she was, but, after all, a girl like that practically asked to be talked about in the wrong way.

"Hi, Etting. You going to a ball?"

Here was Sam Lyons, looking with undisguised amusement at the florist's box. Why in blazes had Helena suggested the library? Deliberately to expose him to this sort of thing? Well, he'd have something to say to her about that. He looked lazily at Sam, managed a real grin, and said, "Intend to have one, anyway."

Sam tactlessly sat down on the bench. "Gotta wait for a book," he explained.

Jay, tightening his jaw, thought an explanation was certainly necessary. Why couldn't the guy wait somewhere else? Why couldn't he go shove his head in a bucket of fission? "How's tricks?" he asked. "How're you coming with your paper?"

"Okay," said Sam. "I've got a brand-new approach. If it works."

"Care to divulge it?" Jay asked with manifest lack of interest.

"Nope. Top secret."

Jay glanced at the clock. Eight-thirty. Precisely one half hour late, and he had gotten here ten minutes early. Who did that girl think she was, anyway? Did she actually think she could keep him hanging around in public places like some dithering freshman? Did she—

"Have to shove," Sam said, getting up. "There's my number on the board."

Jay gave him an impatient flick of the hand, then once again summoned a grin to his lips. "Success to all secrets," he said heartily, and watched Sam walk away. The way people thought you gave a darn about whether they were waiting for books, or writing theses, or had to shove. Lord, most people were conceited. Eight-thirty-five. He was beginning to feel a tumbling anger inside, an actual hostility that now was hard to quell. And then, with a snap of his fingers, he realized what she was doing. Keeping him waiting because of the times he'd done it to her. Paying him back, like a vengeful child.

Helena, of all people. Well, study that, he said to himself, and this time smiled in earnest. Helena, the rational and mature, had proved herself subject first to jealousy and now to vindictiveness.

Oh well, in that light he felt almost tender toward her. She was weak, as girls are and should be. She'd been hurt, and she was trying to pay him back. He'd wait, and when she came, he'd say nothing, not a thing at all. He'd give her this red camellia (*that* would make her feel sheepish) and take her arm, and out they'd go, into the cold night, without a word on the subject of her lateness. If he knew girls, and he did, it wouldn't be long before she'd bring the matter up herself. "You were?" he'd say. "Yes, I guess you were a little late, at that. I was thinking about one thing and another, so the time passed like lightning. Besides, there were . . . oh, nice things to watch. That little blonde—" No, he'd better not say that. "Sam Lyons and I had a long session on our papers, what our angles are going to be—" Show her he had things on his mind besides— He started up as a girl in a beaver coat came hurrying through the doors, and sank back again. Five of nine. I warn you, he told Helena in slow, perfectly formed mental words, I warn you, one minute past nine and I won't be this patient. In fact, one minute past nine and I won't be here at all.

At one minute past he jumped up, choked with fury. Okay, now let her come running with some phony excuse. She won't find me. She'll find this library and that's all. He thought, with angry frustration, of all the time and affection he'd put in on a girl who could pull

111

this sort of stunt. Because of a few broken dates that he couldn't help, and a few times of being late, she'd humiliate him before the whole accursed college, would she? She'd—

The little blonde was coming down the lobby, coat on, fair hair flopping prettily the way long hair did on girls (Helena wore hers too short), books tucked under her arm. Jay half turned away to avoid her, then suddenly turned back.

"*Wie geht's?*" he said, and she halted, turning surprised brown eyes toward him. Brown eyes. That was pretty special. He hadn't noticed that in the house the other night. He was partial to brown-eyed blondes.

"Why . . . why, *auf Wiedersehen,*" she said, and began to laugh. "It's all the German I know."

What a cute piece, he thought, smiling down on her. "I know one other sentence, but it wouldn't get me far on Unter den Linden."

"What is it?"

"*Das ist eine Kuh.*"

"That is . . . this is . . ." She broke off with what Jay considered an adorably puzzled expression.

"This is a cow," he said gravely, and they threw back their heads with laughter.

"Where're you off to?" he asked, casually removing her books from under her arm and replacing them with the white florist's box.

"What—what is this?"

"Now, come. A girl with yellow hair and brown eyes knows what sort of box that is."

"I know. But . . . why are you giving it to me?"

"Because you have yellow hair and brown eyes."

"Well—" She lifted the eyes and gazed into his. "What did I ever do to be so lucky?"

"It's fate. Some are, some aren't. You are. So," he added pointedly, "am I. I got stood up."

"Oh, I don't believe it," she exclaimed, then lowered her gaze. "I mean—"

"I know what you mean," Jay said tenderly. They walked out of the library together. "To get down to fundamentals . . . Name, occupation, destination, in that order, please."

"Nancy Haverman. Student, freshman. And . . . back to the house, I guess. I saw you there the other night, you know. You were waiting for Helena Williams." The question was explicit in her voice.

"I was waiting for her tonight, too," he said, as if it were a fine joke, as, in his opinion, it was turning out to be.

"But she must have gotten hurt, or something," Nancy Haverman said with such sincerity that Jay's heart quite warmed to her.

"Oh, I don't imagine it's that. She's sore at me, is all."

Nancy had the grace not to ask why, and when he suggested they stop by his house, where a coffee dance was in progress (the one to which poor Helena might now be going if she hadn't been so stiff-necked), she hesitated only long enough to wonder about her sweater and skirt.

"You look perfect," he assured her. "Just perfect." He

113

gave her arm a little squeeze and was rewarded with a tremor of her soft body next to his. He wondered what Helena was doing. Sulking somewhere. Well, let her sulk. Let her, he decided, glancing down at the bright head of Nancy Haverman, sulk from now on in.

At home by herself, Helena was not sulking. She was not, either, feeling very happy. This was the only thing she'd been able to think of to make Jay Etting understand finally and for good that she did not care for him. But it was still not a pretty thing to do. Even if he had done it to her on countless occasions—well, countable, but too many by far. The trouble with the scheme was that there was very little chance Jay would think things over calmly and realize that he was only getting one taste of his own extremely unpleasant medicine. More likely that he'd rise up in a spurt of rage and then decide that she was next door to a cretin. Well, anyway, it was done. It was ten o'clock now, and the thing was done.

CHAPTER SIX

ROSEMARY DIDN'T LIKE SAM, BUT EVERYONE ELSE IN THE family did. Within a few days it was accepted, looked for, that Sam Lyons would spend his evenings, not in the master bedroom alone with the peace and quiet he had craved, but in the Reed living room, with whoever happened to be there.

"So what about this being alone, this not wanting distractions, we heard so much about?" Rosemary grumbled to Lenore. "What the heck is quiet and peaceful about sitting around listening to Pop explain how lousy everything is, or Reg describing why the men decided not to go on strike after all? And that's another thing. It just seems funny why Reg likes him, doesn't it?"

"Not especially. You mean you think he should be jealous? How could he be, with the way you act toward Sam?"

Rosemary was bewildered. How had he contrived to deposit himself right in the center of all their activities and make himself welcome there? Before that Saturday they hadn't known him at all, and less than a couple of weeks later he was Sam to everybody and as easily accepted as . . . as Hank. Wandered into the living room in the same at-home way, slouched in a chair looking at television, or talking, or kidding Lenore a little. Having, if not serious, at least sober discussions with Pop. She did not understand it, and she was not resigned. She no longer behaved rudely or sullenly. She certainly never got up and left a room (as she wished to) simply because he'd come into it. But she did not believe his reasons for being here, and she gave nothing of herself when he was present.

They sat now, the five young people (as four of them had used to sit), smoking and talking. The radio was on, very low, and outside a brutish wind raged through the night, rattling windowpanes and threatening the big dying elm beside their house. There had been, earlier, some discussion of the movies, but during dinner the storm had come, unheralded and fierce, and they were surprised that Hank and Reg even made it to the house. There could be no going out. It was, Rosemary thought, turning her ears to it rather than to the voices inside, exciting and terrifying.

She had gone out on the porch, about an hour ago, closing the door behind her and standing close to it, away from the rain. The poor tremendous elm had been in hideous trouble. It had screamed and rocked, and, as she watched, one great bough ripped loose with a splintering wrench, dropped crazily downward, and then hung, swinging and just not falling. An ugly thing to see. Rosemary looked away from it, into the black torrential air. Other trees were suffering, too, flinging their anguished branches about in the wet light from the street lamps. There was almost no traffic. Just now and then a truck or car feeling its way like a blind frightened bug. One of them pulled up to the house, and that had been Reg. He'd come racing up the walk, and pulled to a startled halt to find her on the porch.

"Are you crazy?" he'd demanded. "You wanna get pneumonia or something?"

"You're the crazy one," she'd answered. "To come here at all. Hank did, too. I think you're both crazy."

"And you know who about," he'd grinned, putting an arm about her waist and kissing her lightly. "Come on, let's get in before we're both drenched."

I'd like to go out on the porch again, Rosemary thought now, but of course did not. The minute she made a move Reg would give her his doggedly affectionate orders about what she could and could not do. She did not propose to let Mr. Sam Lyons be witness to that.

"What're you planning to do after high school?" Sam was asking Hank.

"Well," said Hank, leaning forward a little, "I suppose just get a regular job at this place I work week ends, this hardware store. I like it there, and they pay well. And, well—" He shrugged. It was obvious to any listener (and known to Lenore and Rosemary) that the hardware store was not what Hank would choose. But how else could he and Lennie get married if he didn't take a job right away?

"You hadn't thought about college?" Sam asked.

Rosemary's jaw tightened a little. He pried, this boy. He really did. That his voice and his eyes were kindly and filled with interest did not alter the fact that essentially he snooped into all their affairs. And *nobody* seemed to mind. It was incredible. Not only did they not mind, they loved it, expanded under it. She couldn't recall when Pop had so eagerly discussed his thoughts, his old and abandoned ambitions, his money worries. She had never before known Reg to tell anyone but the Reeds about his bank account, his fleet of trucks that would roll one day. He'd even said once, as casually as if to a brother or a well-loved friend, "And of course Rosie and I will be getting married in a couple of years." Why, he hadn't even told *her* that, in so many words. It had been understood (by Reg, not necessarily by her) and that was all. She'd gone scarlet, and Reg hadn't even noticed. Now here was Hank, the most reticent of them all, sitting at the edge of his chair, ready to discuss himself with a stranger.

"Sure. I've thought about it," Hank said. "Who doesn't? But you can't have everything in life, and I want one thing more than any other." He'd glanced at Lenore and their eyes held a moment before he looked away and repeated to Sam, "You can't have everything."

"Not everything, maybe. But . . . some things get worked out. Means waiting, putting things in the right order—or, I should say, a different order—but people do it. Mean to say, waiting a few years when you're young might mean a better life all around for . . . well," he said, coming directly to the point, "for your wife, yourself. The family you'd have."

"I want Hank to go to college, if he can manage it," Lenore said. "I've always wanted him to. But he says no."

Lenore, don't talk to him, Rosemary pleaded silently. Don't you do it, too.

"Then it's up to you to convince him, if you really think it's important," Sam said to Lenore.

"Oh, I do. Rosemary and I have always thought it's the most important thing in the world, haven't we, Rosemary?"

I won't answer, Rosemary thought. She said, "That's putting it a bit strongly, Lenore."

"But, Rosemary—" Lenore burst out.

"Important. Not the most important." She looked away from her sister's startled and then knowing eyes.

"Still," Sam said, "it's something to think over. Especially when you've got a girl who's willing to wait for you."

Rosemary looked at them all with consummate scorn. What's he studying to be, anyway, she said to herself. A psychiatrist? A family counselor? I'll bet they threw him out of that fraternity house for wanting to know too much. And when the end of this month comes, he'll pay up another, and then another, and by the time the term's over we won't have a secret among us. I'd like to ask him a few questions. I'd like to say, Tell me, Mr. Lyons, how much do you pay for your clothes, and do you like your mother, and what shameful memories of your childhood still trouble you sometimes at night? She sighed and listened to the storm and had to admit, to her private mind, the fact that he never did ask rude or very personal questions. Just this constant drawing out of people who were only too happy to be drawn, this patient, ceaseless survey of the way they lived, the things they wanted.

"The thing is," Hank was musing, "that I suppose in a way it could be managed. I mean, my folks could help some. And then I'd have a job week ends, same as now. My grades are good. I could pick up a scholarship, maybe."

"Sounds smart to me," Reg said. "Get you off to a good start, and everything'd be better for you later on."

Lenore's eyes were sparkling. "It'd be fun," she said in a breathless voice. "It would be really fun, Hank. And I could help you with your homework, like I do now," she grinned, and then added to Sam, "not really, you know. Just so we can do it together. And it really wouldn't take too long, not when we'd have something so wonderful to look forward to. And you could—you could be an engineer, Hank. You've always said you'd like to be an engineer."

Hank began to laugh. "Hey, don't talk as if it were all settled. There's a million and one things to work out first." But he sounded excited.

They all, Rosemary thought, are caught up in this thing as if it were the first plan ever made in the world. And what about their other plans? Their sureness that they didn't want to wait for Hank to go through college? Do they discard all that so easily because Sam the Man here tosses a suggestion in the air? I've thought all along that Hank should go to college, and I've said so, but they never listened to me. What does he have, she pleaded with herself, what is it about him that *wins* people so? Only not me. He's going to have one hold-out in this household.

"Rosemary, aren't you listening to me?"

She blinked and looked up to find Reg on his feet. "I said I was going down for Pop," he informed her. "Be back in a few minutes. I got to thinking about him walking home in this storm, and I don't like it."

Rosemary's eyes softened. "I'll go with you," she said, starting to rise.

Reg put firm hands on her shoulders. "Not you, young lady. You stay right here where it's dry and safe. Just wanted to let you know, that's all."

"Want me to come along?" Sam asked.

Reg looked a little surprised. "No," he said. And then, "Thanks, anyway, but I've been getting Pop of a rainy night for years. Don't need any help."

As he went out, Rosemary settled back smiling a little. Reg might talk to Sam Lyons as much as the others did, but he wasn't mesmerized by him, and could put him in his place quite easily when it seemed indicated. She realized that of all of them she was the only one to whom the term "college boy" bore any relation to Sam Lyons. For them, he was someone they all liked (liked too much) talking with. But she was a snob with an inferiority complex. And it's the way I've always been, she thought mournfully. Always, since she could remember, humble before the beautiful houses, the special clothes, the special language. Impressed by people who were part of that world, whether or not they were impressive. Lenore, who admired the college, would have liked to go in order to learn more, as much as to be one of the strolling couples on the tree-canopied campus. But Rosemary only wanted to be *part* of it. She never thought of studies, pictured classrooms in only the vaguest way. What she wanted was to walk into one of those sorority houses and drop her books on a chintz-covered chair and say to another girl, "Do you think you could take a date off my hands this week end, because I seem to find myself with one too many?" She wanted to be part of a snakeline winding across the campus on the night before a big game, singing the college songs lustily, yelling as the big bonfire rose in symbolic entreaty to the gods of good fortune. She wanted to sit, on a winter's night, as girls must be doing this moment, pajamaed ridiculously like the girls in ads, crowded into one lovely bedroom, eating things out of bakery boxes and drinking coffee and talking, talking. . . . *Did you ever in your life see such a bizarre combination as that Corey girl's Bermuda shorts and hoop earrings? Say, anybody know the new Deke, the one with the blue convertible and the convertible blues? Rosemary, want some more cake? Rosemary, could I borrow your yellow jacket? Rosemary . . . Rosemary . . . Rosemary . . .* How they would all talk, and how she would talk with them. She wanted to wander dreamily beside a boy who would wear a thick wool sweater and carry her books. They would shuffle through the crisp brilliance of fallen autumn leaves, and they would talk in soft voices, and be in love with each other, and be going to a tea dance at his fraternity house later in the day. She would have his pin. One of those deeply to be desired, tiny, jewel-like pins with their tiny, infinitely delicate gold chains linked to a golden year. She would wear it all the time, except at night, when the little chain might get broken as she slept. She would put it in a little enamel box at night, on the table beside her bed in her room in her sorority house. She wanted to sit in the springtime beneath the white-starred dogwood trees and think, Well, it's almost over now, but next year . . . next year . . . The ache of longing, and of knowing that what she longed for was impossible, seemed sometimes almost more than any person could bear. I've only had three real feelings in my life, she thought. Losing Mother, knowing Jay, wanting college. Only three, and they've all been painful and none of them ever really leaves me.

"Rosemary, don't you ever listen to anyone any more?" Lenore was asking, a bit impatiently.

"I'm sorry, Lennie. I was listening to the storm, I guess."

Lenore turned her head and looked at a black and rain-splashed window. "It seems to be getting worse," she said, and her voice was suddenly nervous. "Hank you'd better go. You'd better go right now, or your parents will be beside themselves, and so will I."

"Oh, now, it isn't as bad as all that," Hank protested. But he got to his feet. "Maybe it is. I mean, maybe I had better get while the getting's good." He waved to

Sam. "Thanks for putting ideas in my head, boy. Can't tell what might come of them."

"I'll sure want to know," Sam replied, casting an oblique glance at Rosemary and then settling back in his chair as though to listen to the radio.

Hank and Lenore went into the hall, and the closing of the front door came sooner than it generally did. It was immediately reopened by Pop, who came in wet and shivering.

"Got soaked like this, just running from Reg's car," he complained. "It's not a fit night out for a duck, and if that elm stays up, it'll be God's blessing. Been saying all along I oughta have that elm took down, but you know what'd cost?" He seemed to be addressing Sam, shouting from the hall as Lenore helped him off with his overcoat and rubbers. "Cost a cool hundred and fifty, that's what it'd cost. Think they'd give you anything off for good lumber? They will not. Act like they're doing you a favor to even come around and look at it and say okay we'll take it down for a hundred and fifty. Now what'll happen is anybody's guess. Thing's swinging and creaking out there fit to kill, and what I say is, who's it gonna kill?" This amused him sufficiently so that he broke off his monologue, and Lenore hurried to say, "Pop, you'd better get up and take a hot bath, and do it right away. And then you can come down and I'll make you cocoa. Now, please, Pop," she protested, as he came into the living room in his wet shoes. The lower parts of his trousers were drenched, and his shirt front, where he hadn't quite managed to hold the overcoat together, was dark with rain.

"In a minute," he said, and shivered slightly. "Reg says to tell you, Rosie, he'd better get on back while he still could. He's gotta take an early run tomorrow, and he don't want to run a chance on being late. Beats me," he said, scratching his head, "how the boy'll get a truck out on the road tomorrow morning. There's a freeze coming, sure as we're standing here."

"Pop, *no,*" Rosemary cried out. Lenore glanced at her sister, ordinarily so calm about Reg's driving conditions.

"Surest thing you know," Mr. Reed said. "I saw a storm just like this, ten, fifteen years ago. Started out same as this one, rain and wind to beat the devil and come morning it froze over like glass. Not even a cat could walk."

"But they wouldn't let him take a truck out—" Rosemary began.

"These milk trucks run like mailmen. Though, come to think of it, even the mailmen didn't get out that first day. A silver freeze, they called it. Fierce."

"Pop, I said for you to go up and take a bath. You're standing there catching a cold, I tell you."

Mr. Reed turned to Lenore. "Don't push me," he said gruffly, but he started for the stairs, and assented when she asked if he'd be down for cocoa. They could hear his heavy footsteps mount the stairs and cross the hall to the bathroom, hear the sudden rush of water into the tub, hear his plodding progress to his own room, and the door close. They could hear the wind, in an ever-mounting madness, whirl through the night.

Sam, lifting his head, said, "I was in a typhoon once, in Okinawa. Sounded worse than this, but not much."

"Okinawa?" said Lenore. "When was that?"

"After I got out of prep school. I enlisted, and that's where I wound up," he said easily.

I'm only just happening to mention it, Rosemary said to herself. It's just a thing I'm bringing up casually, my silly old war experience. . . .

"What was it like?" Lenore asked. "What did you enlist in, Sam?"

"It was . . . well, the Okinawans seemed to like it. It's a pretty sort of island. Not as pretty as the Japanese main islands, but then I might have been prejudiced. I think Okinawa is a good place to be from. Anyway, that's what we used to say."

You're still saying it, Rosemary thought. She said, "You enlisted, so—"

"I'm not complaining. Just answering questions," he smiled.

"What about the typhoon?" Lenore persisted. "And what branch were you in?"

"In the Navy Air Force. Ground crew. And the typhoon was terrific. No work for four days. Just sat around the quonset with all our stores, food, books, drinks. It was something, all right. Winds between 125 to 165, corrugated iron flapping and flying through the air, everything else flying through the air, no electric lights, water turned off. But it was sort of fun, in a way.

I sat around reading by a kerosene lamp and trying to get the owl to play chess with me."

"Owl?"

"We had house pets. An owl and two puppies. The owl was named Hootmon and was a pretty darn good pet, aside from not playing chess." Sam smiled, shaking his head. "Looked ill-natured, acted ill-natured, loved the puppies, hated people, and was awfully stupid. But a comedian. He gave starts of surprise."

Lenore leaned forward, catching her underlip with pleasure. "Did he, really?"

"Yup. You'd walk into the quonset and Hootmon would hop off his perch with horror, and ruffle. Wouldn't you call that a start of surprise?"

"I sure would," Lenore laughed. "Did you . . . I mean, was it awful, aside from typhoons, I mean?"

"Oh no. Pretty standard stuff, I imagine. I put in two years and was glad to get out. Still, I wouldn't have missed it. One of life's experiences, I suppose." He lost interest and said he thought probably he'd go to bed. "Work to do tomorrow."

"On your thesis, you mean?" Lenore asked.

For some reason he looked away and did not answer immediately. Then he said, "Not exactly. I'm . . . going over to the library to look up some stuff."

"You may not be able to go, if Pop's silver freeze comes back."

"Might not. Well, then I'll read a book and see if I can get someone to play chess with me."

"I don't know how," Lenore said.

"You could learn."

"That'd be fun," Lenore agreed. "Something different, anyway." She glanced at Rosemary, who had picked up a magazine and was reading. "I'll try, anyway."

"Great." Sam got up and stretched. "Well, good night."

" 'Night," said Lenore.

Rosemary looked up. "Oh . . . good night." She returned to her reading until Sam had left the room, then put the magazine down and said with a direct glance at her sister, "What precisely are you doing?"

"Doing?"

"You know what I mean. All this *I'll play chess with you, Sam. Was it terrible in the war, Sam? . . .*"

"Rosemary, will you stop acting like a miffed six-year-old? He's in the house and he's pleasant, and I'm not going to be rude."

"Rude? I wonder Hank doesn't get furious, how unrude you are."

"Hank," Lenore said with dignity, "understands the difference between someone who's being friendly and enjoying another person, and someone who's . . . well, whatever it is you're implying. I think you know, too."

Rosemary dropped her eyes. Yes, she knew all right. Knew that Lenore's friendliness was just that, and her own rudeness just that, too. She also didn't know of a way to stop what she'd begun, and didn't even know that she wanted to. Why should she care, really, what any one of them thought of her behavior? It was only for a month, and then she'd be back the way she used to be. But she could not, even if she tried, be friendly and easy with this member of the enemy.

"I'm sorry," she sighed. "You'll just have to understand, without my telling you anything, Lenore. Because I don't know how to explain it. I only know it is."

For a while they sat in silence, and then the descending tread of their father's feet sent them to the kitchen to prepare his cocoa. Before they could begin, they heard the agonizing split that told them the thing Mr. Reed had feared was happening. They rushed to the front of the house, hearing Sam hurtle down the stairs and out the front door to the porch, where the four of them stood, eyes staring, unable to speak above the wind's fury and the sound of their own hearts' beating, to watch the fall of the dying elm. It seemed to take forever to tear its great roots free from over a hundred years' lodging and lay itself in a grotesquely pitiful, giantly immovable posture across their lawn, the lawn next door, and part way into the street. It fell and fell, slowly because of the huge protesting roots, and with a tremendous sucking, wrenching noise that even the driving rain and wind could not obliterate. It caught in its boughs wires that meant light and communication and dragged them tangling downward, and, at last, with an earth-shaking thud, lay down, branches cracking and tossing. As it hit the earth, all the lights on the street went out.

It was, for a few moments, too difficult to grasp. The tree lay there across the lawns and sidewalk, but surely the tree still stood? It must. It had stood there, in that place, longer than all their ages put together, longer than the sidewalks had been here, or the houses, so the tree could not just be thrown across earth and pavement. Yet, there it lay, a black form in the now totally black and rain-filled night.

Mr. Reed shuddered and said numbly, "This'll take every penny I have. This'll break me, getting that thing out of the street."

"Don't you have insurance, sir?" Sam asked.

"Insurance? I have a little insurance on the shop, that's all. Nothing to cover this. I should have had it done before. I should have—" He turned to the door with a baffled groan, realized there was no light, and said, "Got a match, Sam? We'd better find some candles somewhere. If we got any candles."

"There are a few, Pop," Rosemary told him. Her voice was hushed, as though they were all in mourning.

They made their way soundlessly, by touch, through the dark house to the dining room. "In here, somewhere," Rosemary whispered, moving with her arms outstretched to the sideboard drawers. It seemed ages before her fingers closed on a cool round column, but at length she had two candles. "The kitchen," she directed, and they followed, Sam tripping over a chair, where she led. In the kitchen, the pilot light of the stove made a tiny purple flame, disembodied in the darkness. It looked, Rosemary thought, as though it might be the last light in the world after a deluge, after an annihilating war.

"Well, come on, come on," Lenore said impatiently,

and Rosemary moved toward the little point of fire, just as Sam struck a match. She turned, holding the candle to him.

"I didn't think of that," she said. "All I could remember was the pilot light."

As the wick caught, the flame lit his face. He was not handsome in the manner of Jay Etting, who looked like a lot of other handsome boys. He was different, himself, not a duplicate of anyone. Older than many of the boys at college, because he'd started later. She noticed all this, nettled somewhat at noticing, dropped her glance, and lit the other candle. "I'll find holders for these," she said. "Then maybe we can find some more someplace."

"Be a run on candles tomorrow," Mr. Reed said. "Won't be a one left in the store by noon."

"Well, be sure you set some aside for us," Lenore said, just as Rosemary said, "You won't be able to get to the store tomorrow, Pop."

Mr. Reed grunted and did not reply directly. "No telling when they'll get the lights going. I remember last time it was three days before they got the electricity on again all over town, and your mother said even if the coal furnace was a darn nuisance most of the time, this time we were luckier than other people. She was right, too. All the folks with oil burners darn near froze to death. Going around in their overcoats all the time, crawling up next the fireplaces. And we've got a gas stove, too. Plenty of people with electric stoves'll wish they'd never bought them, let me tell you, by the time *this* blow is over." He sounded almost pleased, as if for once he was coming out on top. He so rarely did come out on top that his good fortune in this respect seemed for a moment to have taken his thoughts off the tree and its necessary removal. How will we manage that? Rosemary wondered, and then tried to put it out of her mind, too.

"This is sort of fun," Lenore said suddenly. "I hope we get marooned." She sighed, and Rosemary could feel her wishing she hadn't ordered Hank home so quickly, and then he could have been marooned with them. "Could I have one of those candles?" Lenore asked, taking one. "Back in a sec."

"What are you going to do?" Mr. Reed called plaintively. "Where are you going?"

"To see if the phone works," Lenore called over her shoulder, and she went, a drifting, eerily lit figure, into the hall. They could hear her pick up the receiver, hear her dial, stop, dial again, finally replace the phone and start back. "Dead," she said. "Rosemary, what will I do now? How do I know he got home at all, with trees falling and so much rain and all? How am I going—"

"There's nothing you can do," Sam interrupted. "Not tonight. But he left pretty early, and he's a competent guy. I don't think you have to worry about either of those fellows. They know what they're doing."

Rosemary moved uneasily, and said she'd try to find a candle for each of them and that then they'd better go to bed.

"Who're you telling to go to bed?" Mr. Reed grumbled, but he yawned and took his candle and moved off wearily. Lenore and Rosemary looked after him, and then at each other.

"How much do you think it does cost, Sam?" Lenore asked.

"Removing the tree? I don't know. I could find out for you."

"Oh, we'll find out soon enough," Rosemary said. She was tired, and they were going to have to find money and did not know how much, and she did not, like Lenore, find this fun.

Lying in bed, after Lenore had fallen asleep, she became aware of something unnatural. Something that made her turn restlessly and stare into the darkness of the room as though to find an answer. What had happened? She lay tensely, listening, turning her head. Then, almost with a sensation of fright, she realized that it was the silence she'd recognized. The wind was gone, and the rain, and there wasn't even the splash and drip from the gutters that should follow such a storm. Shivering, she pulled her bathrobe around her and moved cautiously to the window. It was closed and she couldn't see a thing, but the glass was a sheet of ice, and it seemed to Rosemary that the night was tragically, frozenly quiet.

Pop's silver freeze.

She heard her father go down in the morning to stoke the furnace. Sometimes she heard him, sometimes did not, but rarely did she get up before at least a small tendril of warmth had found its way up from the cellar. This morning she took her clothes to the bathroom, so as not to waken Lenore, and dressed there, shivering. She held her wrists under the hot water for a while, closing her eyes with pleasure at the way it warmed her arms and even her back. I'll never hate that coal furnace again, she told herself. She didn't see how anyone could survive hours and days of a house from which all the warmth had leaked away. The cold would press through the walls, under the sills, it would sift through the rooms with its gradual touch, till everything was hard and stony, the linen on the beds, the rugs on the floors, the hands and ankles of people trying to endure. I just couldn't, she thought. I'd have to set the house on fire, just to keep warm. She felt almost joyous, going downstairs, because their furnace was down in the cellar doing its job.

And there was Pop, blinking and stretching, waiting for his coffee to percolate. He nodded at her and then, to her surprise, spoke. "Did you look outside yet?"

She shook her head. "I ran straight for the kitchen. I've been thinking about what it would be like to wake up this morning to a house you couldn't heat."

They glanced with devotion toward the cellar door.

"Just goes to show," said Mr. Reed, "that you don't always know who your friends are." He rubbed his eyes. "I'm tired, Rosie. And I don't see how I can make it down to the store at all today."

"Is it that bad?"

"Take a look."

Rosemary started for the kitchen door, changed her mind, and went down the hall to the front. She'd have to look at the fallen giant sometime, and see just how gigantic it was, so it might as well be now.

Sam came down the stairs as she reached for the knob.

"Good morning," she said, turning slightly.

"Morning—" For a moment it seemed that he would add Rosemary, and she realized that they never did address each other by name, but all he said was, "Have you seen it yet?"

"I was just going to."

"Well, be prepared for something. I looked out my window and it's breath-taking. Only be careful, because the porch is probably a pane of ice. Mind if I come along?"

Rosemary didn't look at him, but she said surely, if he wished to, and they stepped into the storm entrance of the porch and opened the storm door. Then they simply stared.

"Told you so," Sam said, after a bit.

It was quite impossible to walk on the porch. It would be impossible, Rosemary thought in stunned silence, to walk anywhere today at all. A world that had rejected man, wrecked his communications, defied him to emerge from his puny shelters, that had torn up its own trees, eroded its own earth, now lay in icy retreat, remote and unapproachable. It had the unreal, untrustworthy beauty of death as it sparkled and refracted color from every glass-taut broken wire, every branch and twig and crouched, frozen automobile. The lawn was ragged under its cover of ice, the pillars of the porch were shining frozen columns, and the roots of the great elm sprayed upward like a marble waterfall.

Rosemary shivered, and Sam said, "We'd better go in."

"Oh, it isn't the cold," she answered vaguely, but she followed him into the house and shut the door.

Mr. Reed, chin on his fist, stared at the kitchen floor and said as they entered, "I won't be able to get down to the store today. I just don't see any way to get down there at all."

"Not a chance, sir," said Sam. "But I guess nobody would come even if you did manage it."

"They'll be wanting candles. Somebody'll manage to get there. Might even break in," he added gloomily.

Rosemary stifled an impulse to laugh. "Oh, Pop, no. Don't worry like that. Why don't you pretend it's a holiday and just enjoy it?" Her father looked up in unconcealed astonishment. "Well, anyway," she added quickly, "since you can't get there, you might as well forget about it."

Mr. Reed grunted and got up for another cup of coffee. "Rosie," he said, "somewhere in the cellar there's a couple of kerosene lamps, and kerosene, too. Be a good girl and find them after you eat." His disconsolate voice would not now admit their fortune in a coal furnace, candles, a couple of kerosene lamps and kerosene to go in them. "You see that tree?" he inquired of Sam. "Tore down the telephone wires, you noticed. Of course, the telephone people take care of their own stuff, acts of God or something, I won't have to pay for that. But the tree! *Why* didn't I have it cut down before?"

"Because you couldn't afford it," Rosemary said briskly.

"I can't afford it now, but there it is, all over the sidewalk and street."

"So now you afford it. Some things just can't be gotten around, and that tree is one of them." She was breaking eggs for scrambling, and so did not see the querulous look her father sent her. A treacherous, beautiful world out there, she thought, and it was going to cost a great many people a great deal of money they could not afford. Pop wasn't the only one, even if he'd like to think so. There was a poem she'd read once in high school, and though as a rule she did not remember poetry, two lines of this one had remained with her because they seemed so real. *"Oh, little 'tis the luck I've had, and ah, 'tis comfort small, to think that many another lad has had no luck at all."*

And that about describes it, she thought, putting toast and eggs in front of Sam. That several people up and down the street were as badly or worse off than the Reeds had not occurred to her father, and did not comfort her.

"People are awfully hard to please," she said now, sitting down to the table, hooking her heels on the rung of the chair.

"Please?" said her father. He turned the word around

137

as if it were an unopened letter. "What's there to be pleased about?"

Rosemary had no answer, nor, it seemed, did Sam.

Lenore, coming in at that moment, glanced from one face to another and then said anxiously, "Do you think Hank got home all right? How would I *know*, with no telephone?"

"It isn't going to do you a bit of good, fussing this way," Rosemary said. "Hank has always been able to take care of himself, and you know it." She watched pride contend with worry in her sister's face. "Hank knows what to do, and how to do it," she persisted. "And he wouldn't want you upset."

Her tactics seemed to work. Lenore, at any rate, began to eat with the rest of them, and was able to talk about the freeze. "It looks like the end of the world," she informed them. "Like the Arctic. Like hell must look. I'm sure hell is a frozen place, and not hot at all—" She talked volubly and then, with a start of delight, sprang from her chair. "Hank!" she called, rushing to the kitchen door and flinging it open. "Hank, how in the world . . . Oh, darling, are you frozen? Whatever made you—" She pulled a cold-reddened, laughing Hank into the kitchen, patting his shoulders and dancing around him like a kitten. "You're incredible," she told him. "Just the most incredible—"

"Hold on," Hank laughed, giving her a quick squeeze and then looking around at the rest of them, who sat stupefied in their places. "See?" he said, pointing to his feet and waving his hands. "It was easy. Well, not to say easy," he grinned at Lenore. "Isn't everyone could do it, but—"

He had a ski pole in each hand, on his feet were a pair of heavy, cleated football shoes. He wore a thick parka, ski pants, leather gloves. He looked cold and pleased with himself and enormously good-humored.

Mr. Reed, looking at this apparition, grimaced. "You forget," he muttered. "You forget what young people can do. You forget even what it's like." He shook his head, as though trying to remember, and then apparently gave up.

He wants to get to his store, Rosemary thought, as much as Hank wanted to get to Lenore, but he won't be able to, because he's old. And she wondered, almost for the first time, what it was going to be like, getting older, and then older, and then finally old. Too old even to do what you wanted to, let alone what you did not. Yet people managed the last, didn't they, long after they'd abandoned the first? In the store there were tired women who didn't want to work, but had to and did. How many times had she heard one of them say, Oh, I'd have liked to go there, to see that, to do this, but I was just too tired . . . I couldn't. Too tired to do what you'd like. But you can't be too tired to do what you must. She looked at her father and felt a painful kind of tenderness for him. He worked and he worried and he got grumpy. But once he was as young as Hank, and strong enough to do incredible things, strong enough to dream. Once he was in love and had a life before him. Now he had a candy store he couldn't get to, and a tree he couldn't afford to get rid of, and he couldn't even remember what it had been like being young. Unconsciously, she sighed.

"Anything I can do?" Sam asked. Everyone else was talking, and the question, directed solely to Rosemary, gave her a startling effect of closeness to him. She turned his way with widened eyes, and then lowered her glance quickly. "I just meant," he went on, "that you seemed sort of sad, and I wondered if I could help." His young voice was so deep, his eyes so amazingly gentle.

"Oh, no. Thank you. I seem to think things that make me sigh." But what am I thinking now, she thought, what in the world am I thinking now?

For a moment he continued to study her face, and then gave her a slow smile before he turned to Hank and said, "How was it, really, coming over?"

"Rugged," said Hank, accepting coffee and sitting down to remove his shoes. "In spite of all her chatter, I don't believe Lenore, here, nearly appreciates the difficulties and dangers I've undergone. No provisions, no human contact—"

"No sense," Lenore put in.

"That's right. I had nothing. But I made it, and I want you to jot it down in your diary tonight, Lennie, in case some day you think I'm neglecting you."

"I don't keep a diary."

"Well, start one."

"All right," said Lenore, and for a moment she and

Hank looked at each other as if they were alone, and then forced their glances apart.

And she probably will start one, Rosemary thought. She would do anything in the world Hank asked her to. It was a good thing that Hank was the person he was, and would not ask too much. But, looking at them, Rosemary felt again the wrench of longing to be as they were, to be in love. I'll never have it, she thought wildly. I'll have Reg and his devotion, or people like . . . people like Jay Etting. She held her arms close to her body, squeezing away from the memory, and wondered, suddenly, if Sam Lyons knew Jay. Her cheeks stung, wondering what Jay might have said about her, since that night, to the people he knew. I don't care, really, she assured herself. Even if he'd mentioned me to Sam, I wouldn't care.

Even?

She got up nervously and said she'd go down and look for the kerosene lamps. When Sam made a gesture of rising, she waved him back.

"No, thanks very much, but I can find them easily," she said, and fled the kitchen.

CHAPTER SEVEN

"ROXANNE."

"Huh?"

"Come over here and look at this."

Roxanne walked to the window, looked out, and whistled. "Lordy. We're done for. Nobody'll get out of this alive."

They gazed across the campus, the glass-shrouded, glistening, soundless, and motionless campus.

"It's the fourth glacial period," Roxanne decided, "snuck up on us in the night. Or is it the third?"

"Don't they fossilize everything living?"

"Oh, no. Just wipe out a few species. I think we're about due for wiping out, don't you?"

"You sound like Anne. But she's going to be disappointed. She expected us to be blown up, not cooked in a deep freeze."

"Cooked in a deep freeze," Roxanne repeated. "What is that supposed to mean?"

"Oh, well," Helena said vaguely. She leaned forward, holding her breath so as not to cloud the pane. No, not

142

a person stirring, not a vestige of movement, not a shadow of sunlight. Shadow of sunlight . . . What in the world had gotten into her this morning? Working on the paper for Mr. Warner, possibly. She was thinking so much about words lately that she'd addled her brain. That was it. She was working, now, on a section dealing with the peculiar way different words came into style, so to speak. Like equate. People didn't used to say equate, they said liken, or the same as, or even compare —though that was incorrect. But now you didn't say subversion and liberalism are not the same thing. You said don't equate subversion with liberalism. And osmosis. Used to be strictly for the laboratory, but now every baby knew that a thing didn't dawn on you, or gradually become, it happened through osmosis. And the way words changed. A smear used to be what got on the floor when you dropped your bread and jam, but now it was what happened to people who got called up before investigating committees. Funny thing. Only sometimes, of course, not funny at all. She continued to stare at a world entombed in crystal, and at length turned away.

In the dining room, half an hour later, Mrs. Mack, the housemother, tapped on her glass for attention.

"I observe," she said, "that many of you girls are dressed for going out." She looked around the room, where fully half the girls were outfitted in ski suits and heavy boots. The other half, like Helena, had apparently already decided that no classes would be attended or even held today, and had dressed for staying in. It was awful to think how much studying you could get done today, if you really applied yourself. Helena had a notion that few people would. There was a holiday spirit here among the cornflakes and poached eggs, and who wanted to spend an unexpected holiday doing what she ought to do? Mrs. Mack was going on. "I am sorry to have to say that no one is to leave the house until some sort of thaw has set in. We've scattered ashes on the porch and sidewalk, but aside from that there's nothing to do but wait. I cannot have you risking your necks on these streets this morning." She glanced about to quell a murmur of protest. "I'm sorry," she repeated.

"Makes sense, I suppose," Helena said to Roxanne, scowling beside her.

"But I wanted to sit down and slide to the Beta house to see how they'd been taken."

"Same as us, dear, I'm sure. Anyway, wait until they slide to you. It's more maidenly."

"They can't slide uphill," Roxanne pointed out in an aggrieved voice.

"Then how did you plan to get back?"

"I didn't," Roxanne giggled.

"We are fortunate," Mrs. Mack was going on, "in that our electricity and phone are unaffected. Some parts of the town are completely without either service, but please do not, unless it is absolutely necessary, make use of the telephone. The operators are frantic now, and frivolous telephoning will only make their work more difficult." She studied her empty plate, nodded as if in answer to herself, and said, "That, I think, will be all. Naturally, you are aware that this un-expected day indoors would provide an excellent opportunity for work on your assignments." This last sentence was spoken automatically and elided with her, "If you'll excuse me now," as she left the table. It was clear that Mrs. Mack, however unreal her syntax, was realistic in her knowledge of the girls.

Upon her departure, conversation in the room burst like spray from a Fourth of July sparkler. Helena, listening to it, thought that a room full of feminine voices sounded like nothing else in the world but a roomful of feminine voices. A unique and universal noise, and not, she thought, an unpleasant one. If you didn't have to hear it too often, that was.

"I have to phone my mother," she said to Roxanne. "I wouldn't call that a frivolous use of the phone, would you? Mom'll be worried if I don't."

"I have to phone the Beta house," Roxanne muttered, "and that—"

"Wait till he phones you. Whoever he is. Who is he, by the way?"

"Johnston Bailey."

"Oh? Since when?"

"Met him a couple of weeks ago, at a coffee dance they gave," Roxanne said casually. She turned a quick eye on Helena. "That one I told you about, only you probably didn't listen."

"You mean the one Jay took Nancy Haverman to?"

"Very same."

"I was listening. I just didn't pay much attention to who you were with."

"Whom. Flattering, aren't you?"

"I never flatter my good friends. Thereby flattering them all the more. I don't think you should call him."

"You don't think I really meant to, do you?"

"I don't see why it would be such an awful thing to do."

Roxanne got up, laughing. "I'm going to change, since we've been immured. See you upstairs."

Helena, after calling her mother, went up to the room to find Roxanne cleaning her dresser drawers. She had everything ranged about her in great disorder and was studying the result despondently.

"I pulled it all out quickly," she explained, "so I wouldn't be able to get away with doing just one drawer."

"Want me to help?"

"Oh, no. These are all my intimate things, and I intend to have a place for everything. From now on, a place for everything. Then I'll know where everything is, see?"

"And then?"

"Then I'll be able to get up fifteen minutes later in the morning, when I know that the slips aren't in the shoe bag and my hairbrush in someone's room down the hall. A little order is a valuable thing." She folded a blouse carelessly and stuffed it in the bottom drawer. "Blouses here," she said to herself. "Must remember that the blouses will be in here." She glanced up. "Are you ever going to tell me what happened about you and Jay that night?"

"It's not especially interesting."

"You'd be surprised what I find interesting. Give."

Helena sat in a chair, lit a cigarette, let the match burn almost to her fingertips before blowing it out.

"I couldn't seem to make him understand," she said carefully, "that I really was sick of the whole business. Of going out with him, and having him flirt all over the map with anything that struck his fancy. I've told you all this before."

"Yes, but not about the night of the coffee dance. I want to hear that part."

"I told him to meet me at the library, and then I went home and went to bed."

Roxanne looked appalled. "You mean you actually *did* that? I can imagine—I guess I can imagine—thinking of such a thing, but I never in the world could do it. I just wouldn't be able to stay away, knowing he was waiting. It's . . . it's hideously rude."

"He hadn't been precisely gallant to me."

"I know, but—" Roxanne clucked slightly. "And Nancy had a camellia on that night, did I tell you? She went out of her way to tell me that Jay had given it to her, so of course he got it for you. She isn't awfully bright, is she? Did she think I'd actually believe he'd bought it for her? But doesn't it make you feel awful to think of him sitting there with that camellia, waiting and waiting for you? I'd die."

"I wouldn't. I'm not even touched. You don't know

Jay the way I do. The camellia was to make me feel ashamed of myself."

"For what? He didn't know you'd be late when he got it."

"For being so evasive about making the date. I put it off too long. Jay does not like to be put off."

"Well, but—" Roxanne sat back on her heels. "You really are astounding, Helena."

"I don't think so. I have some pride, but that shouldn't be so astounding."

"It sort of leaves you without dates at all, for the time being, doesn't it?" When Helena didn't reply, she added, "Most of the girls think Nancy took him away from you."

"I'm sure they do, if Nancy has anything to say about it. You know, she and Jay should get along fine. They're so much alike. They both have a way of putting words in other people's mouths and motives in other people's emotions. Jay spread it all around that I was so jealous of him I practically carried a machete to beat off the competition, and there wasn't any way to stop him. But I think he's met his match in young Nancy."

"If flirting has anything to do with it, he has. She'd make a dead-set at a lamppost, if someone had hung a pair of pants on it." Roxanne folded stockings together. "I don't like stockings that are rolled up and then tucked inside each other, do you? It looks . . . underprivileged, somehow. As if you only had one pair. I have three, if that run doesn't go below the knee. You know, that's something I couldn't stand—having some other girl take charge of a boy I used to have. I mean, having a right to talk about him and say what he's doing or thinking. Even when I was a kid I was like that. I didn't want them, but I didn't want someone else to have them either."

"What did you do about it?"

"Oh, there isn't always anything you can do, but I used to get interested in a boy all over again the minute I found somebody else was. Very wrong of me, of course," she added smoothly.

"Not a unique reaction. The thing is, with Jay I'm so relieved not to have to bother any more that I just don't care. I wish Nancy the joy of him." She stood up and wandered to the window. "Mother says it's the same over there, *sheeted* with ice and not a creature stirring." She fiddled with a string on the blind and said moodily, "Funny, how they call it Mother Nature. Mothers aren't like this . . . captious and unreliable. And unkind."

"I imagine some of them are."

"I mean the conception of the word, generally. And most mothers aren't. This Nature creature seems to me like some old fumbling sexless thing that doesn't know the reason for most of its actions, or even know that it's acting at all a good deal of the time. Like an old bear in a coma, shifting around and causing havoc in the undergrowth, but not *knowing* about it." She turned back to the room. "What are you going to do today? Study?"

"I'm going to finish this," Roxanne said, casting a slit-like glance at the task she'd set herself. "And then I thought we could go downstairs and all be girls together. Get a taffy pull organized, or build a fire and sit around listening to Eddie Fisher and darkening a few reputations. Something innocent and feminine, like. For instance, did you know that Penny Wortley has been climbing in and out of the window of her sorority for ages? At night. She has a window near—"

"I thought that sort of thing had gone out of date. Girls in nineteenth-century novels climbed out of boarding school windows and it was all very dashing. But these days . . . Doesn't it strike you as sort of—quaint?"

Roxanne looked up with a nettled expression. "You know, Helena, there aren't many people could tolerate you as a roommate. You're too cool and respectable."

Helena laughed. "I'm sorry. I'll try to disgrace myself. In some *very* girlish and reprehensible way. I'll elope with Bub Holden."

"Gee, kid," Roxanne said in a deep, resounding voice, "gee, I'd liketa, but Coach says I gotta be a example to the other fellas, gotta stay in trainin', like . . . gosh, kid—"

"Another hope down the drain," Helena sighed, and dropped to the floor beside Roxanne. "Here, I'll fold and you put away. Otherwise we'll be stepping around your effects for the rest of the term."

In the afternoon Mr. Reed, who could not be consoled for missing a day at his store, trudged off to the upper part of the house. "To take a nap," he said dully.

And he'll lie there, Rosemary thought, and go on

brooding. Poor Pop, poor stubborn tired Pop. This must be a thing that runs in our family, she told herself, this inability to accept what is already a fact. In Lenore it comes out as a sort of hopefulness, but in Pop and me it's just . . . mulishness. Over and over Pop had moaned at his failure to have the tree cut down in time. Down it was, sprawling before his eyes, but he seemed to feel that if he talked enough, sorrowed enough, somehow the tree would be standing once again and he would have the chance back to have it decently, more cheaply, sawed down. When the fact was, she realized, that if by some miracle the tree did stand up again, Pop would be the first to find a reason for not doing a thing about it. "Stood this long, hasn't it? And I ain't got the money, that's the long and short of it. It's too expensive, this getting trees sawed down. We'll just have to take a chance." Yes, that's what Pop would say, as she, in spite of hindsight and remorse and the knowledge of danger, found herself once again falling in love and unable to prevent it. With Sam Lyons. Though she had so disliked and resented him, in a few hours she had woven him into the pattern of her life. As she had, so many times in the past, for no understandable or enduring reasons, woven this one and that till it seemed that her own pattern would be obscured entirely and nothing remain but a tapestry of a new boy's face. And why this time? she wondered. Because the leaping candlelight had touched his features in a certain way. Because his voice, for a moment, had seemed warm and protective. So she had looked at him in a new fashion, and could not look away. Oh, not literally. She avoided his glance, kept her own voice free of warmth. And every moment she was aware of him, every moment longed to hear him speak, to see him enter a room, to realize with dazed sweetness that he still would be with them for two weeks, and then would grow chilled to know that in two weeks he'd be gone.

Please, she begged herself, please, please, make sense. You have gone through this before. You know what the longing is, the ache, the bounding betraying happiness. You *know* all that. Please be sensible. Recognize this for what it is, another self-deception, another infatuation. You aren't in love, you've never been in love. *Nobody* could be in love as often as you have known you were, as quickly, and as frantically, as . . . pridelessly. Think about the time you loved that young policeman, and thought about him at night, and flushed when he spoke to you in the street. That was all he ever did, say a friendly word, and look like Apollo in a uniform, and that was all you needed to feel you were in love for nearly two months. You got over it. Got over the boys in high school, the young man in the haberdashery department at the store, that friend of Reg's who came here with him a few times and kidded you and moved away to Philadelphia. Some of them loved you, or thought they did, or said they did. Some of them you kissed, and some, like the minister's brother, you never even spoke to. But it was all part of the same thing, she told herself fiercely. All part of nothing, and you're a fool. Oh God, she thought, dropping her head to her hands, such a fool.

"Head ache?" Sam asked, coming into the living room, where Rosemary had been sitting alone.

She looked up quickly, helpless to repress the leaping of her heart, maintaining, just barely, steadiness in her eyes and voice. A fool, a fool. "A little bit. It's been—distracting."

"Yes, I know." He sat in a chair opposite and turned his head thoughtfully to one side. "I've been thinking, Rosemary—"

Rosemary. The first time he'd called her that. And presently she'd be able to call him Sam. Sam had never seemed a nice name before, never a name she would have picked for—for anyone. But Sam, Sam . . . His head was shaped so nicely, and his hands. He was so easeful and low-voiced . . .

"Miss Reed, you aren't listening to me."

"I was . . . I'm sorry, I was thinking about something," she said cautiously.

"That's understandable. A thing like this happens and it's bound to drive all other things out of your mind. Thing is, what I have in mind relates to your father's problem . . . Oh, hi, Hank. How's the dinner going?"

"Lenore says I'll never be a cook, praise be. I'm the kind of guy who'd be glad to do the dishes or walk the baby, but whipping up a meal out of a teaspoon of spinach and an empty can of baking powder is just out of my line."

He sounds so domesticated, so working-class domesticated, Rosemary thought, and was sickened with scorn for herself. This was what happened to her. She betrayed loyalties, watching the pattern of a boy's face. If she were still in love with the policeman, Hank would have sounded touching, even witty, because the policeman might say much the same thing. But Sam Lyons did not come of a family where men were required to do dishes or help with the cooking, if they were nice men, or scorn such work if they were not. Sam simply wouldn't think in such terms. She realized she did not know in what terms he'd think, nor, in fact, what sort of family he came from. But you can guess those things, she told herself. You can tell by the phrasing, the clothes, the references made or not understood, according to their place in his life. You can—

"I've been trying to get Rosemary here to listen to me for two consecutive minutes," Sam was saying, "but she keeps drifting off on some stream of her own."

"Rosemary has her own thoughts. Like all of us."

And not all of them too good to be true, she thought, wishing Hank would not sound protective.

"Reg says," Hank went on, "that half the time when *he's* talking to her, she blanks out, like someone in a dream."

Now why did he have to bring Reg into the conversation? With that emphasis that made her sound like Reg's property. Leave Reg out of this, will you, she demanded silently and resentfully. Don't remind Sam of Reg, don't mention him at all. Or how will Sam . . .

"What were you saying . . . Sam?" she asked. "I'm

sorry, but I do that with everybody." She emphasized the everybody. "Down at the store, I sometimes—" She dropped that. "You were saying, anyway?"

Sam grinned. "You're a funny girl," he said, and the response to a personal remark stirred in her fatally. "Well," he went on, not noticing the effect he had on her, since all her artful being was bent on concealing it, but rather pleased to find that for the first time he had won some sort of attention from the cool "elder Reed," as he called her to himself. "Well, it's about this tree."

"Boy, if you've got any ideas on that, trot them out," Hank said fervently. "The thing's going to drive Mr. Reed batty." Lenore came in at that moment, sniffing her fingers. "Too much onion, baby?" he inquired, patting the sofa beside him. "I can't take them at all," he explained to Sam. "Had to fly the kitchen in tears. Beats me how women can fix the things at all, though, gosh knows, I love them. Raw, fried, smothered—"

"Something needs smothering," Lenore said. She turned to her sister. "Rosemary, I can't find a blessed thing but canned hash and canned frankfurters and some leftover beans out of a can. Oh, and the onions, of course, and Jell-O, but if this thing keeps up—"

"I don't know whether anybody's interested," Rosemary cut in, "except me, that is, but for the past fifteen minutes Sam has been trying to say just one thing and people keep on interrupting—" Aware that her voice was growing shrill, she made an attempt to recapture her lost poise. "That is, first of all I kept getting dreamy, thinking about . . . the tree and when the freeze will end and all—"

"Well, who's interrupting now?" Hank put in. He scratched his head briefly, gave Rosemary a curious glance, and she subsided into silence.

The silence lengthened, and then Hank and Sam began to speak simultaneously, simultaneously quieted, and started up again.

"You," Hank shouted. "You talk."

"Well, it's this way," Sam said warily. "That tree out there is dead as a doornail, practically, but a lot more inflammable, under the right conditions. So my idea is to call the guys at the Deke house and suggest that if they get over here posthaste with a saw or two, the minute the thaw sets in, we could have enough firewood to keep that hearth of ours blazing for the rest of the year and most of next. Since you don't have a fireplace here, it wouldn't be any use to you, and this way you'd get the thing carted away for free." He looked around at them. "How's it strike you?"

Lenore leaped up, flung her arms around his neck, and planted a kiss on the top of his head. "It strikes me that you're Santa Claus and Einstein wrapped up in a pancake."

"I'd do the same myself, boy, do the same myself, if it would become us," Hank said. He looked at Lenore. "However, you've gotten your point over beautifully. Don't labor it. Get back here."

"What do you think, Rosemary?" Sam asked.

I love you, she thought. I really do. Anyone would

have to love you. "I think it's . . . the most wonderful and thoughtful idea I've ever heard of."

"That's how I hoped you'd all feel," Sam said comfortably. "So now all we have to do is wait for a thaw and wait for the telephone to work again."

"Do you really think they'll do it?" Lenore asked. "It seems like such a big job."

"Not a doubt in the world," said Sam.

"How'll you get the wood over to your house, though?"

"Why, I thought probably Reg could borrow a truck somehow," Sam replied, as though he were sure of the answer. Sure of all the answers, Rosemary thought, and now it only made him more to be desired.

Lenore got to her feet. "I have a little more to do about dinner. You want to help?" she asked her sister.

"Oh, of course." Rosemary realized she hadn't done a thing all day except stand at the windows to see the silver freeze, or wander about dazedly in the puzzle of this newest love. "Of course, Lennie. I'm sorry."

Lenore smiled. "Not much to do, sweetie. You can set the table." In the kitchen, she eyed her sister closely. "Anything wrong, Rosemary?"

How often people say that to me, Rosemary thought. Anything wrong? I have the kind of face that looks sad if there is nothing directly to be happy about. Even if I'm not sad, I look it. Lenore, when she's peaceful or not immediately reacting to something, looks serene. Pop looks worried. I look sad. I think Mom used to look sad, too. Only with a difference—a fondness, or something, in her eyes. She sighed, and looked at her sister, and shook her head. "What would be wrong? No, nothing at all, Lennie."

"That's good." Lenore did not seem quite convinced, but when she next spoke it was of Hank. "He's going to sleep on the sofa in the living room tonight, okay? He told his folks . . ."

"Do you have to say folks?" Rosemary said, more sharply than she'd intended.

"Why . . . why, no, not if it bothers you," Lenore said slowly. "He told his people that he wouldn't be home tonight, on account of—" Her voice trailed away and she moved to the stove, stirring vigorously at a barbecue sauce.

"Lenore, I'm sorry."

"Oh, that's all right."

But she did not turn around, nor address her sister again until they were all seated at the kitchen table, and then only indirectly.

Rosemary ate in silence. There was nothing she could do now. It was too late, as it had been too late so many times before. You don't live down your mistakes, she thought suddenly. Your mistakes wear you down, but don't get downed themselves. I've been through all this before, she told herself, and here I'm about to go through it again, and I can't stop. *Going through it again* seemed strangely, chillingly, like being at the beginning of a tunnel. You knew what to expect, you did not wish to travel there, but willy-nilly in you went, and they called it the tunnel of love.

She ate silently, in an intense awareness of Sam. Of the way he tipped his chin in the air when he was thinking, of the fineness of his wrists turning in the cuffs of his green plaid shirt, and the movement of his muscles beneath the shirt. Of his voice and his eyes and his nearness. A fool, a fool, I met a fool in the kitchen. That was a misquotation from a play they'd given in high school long ago, when she had been in love with someone but could not, now, remember whom.

She woke in the middle of the night to a sound of stirring and splintering, to a steady, heavy drip, drip in the darkness. The thaw had come. Some—what would they call it on the radio?—some warm air mass was moving in upon them, bringing thaw. Massively warm it must be, she realized, listening to the tremendous stir and melting in the night. She got quietly out of bed, pulling on her robe, and went to the window. The street lights were glowing. So those awe-inspiring men who worked in the cold and the dark, no matter what the hour, no matter if other people slept or woke, had been out again, working their wonders, and the lights were going. In their wet gleam she could see how the streets had melted into dark flowing rivers, the lawns turned slushy and broken. From the shining jet branches of trees the water ran and fell, dripping in fringes, steadily, hastily. Above her eye level, from the eaves, great icicles dribbled like solvent cones, and as she watched, one glistening spear detached itself and plunged downward. She heard it strike the walk and chime and burst. A truck came down the street, flashing a blinker that fluttered the air with crimson, throwing little combers of water to either side of its wheels. An emergency repair truck of some sort, speeding casually but certainly to the place of emergency. She watched until its stuttering beacon was cut off by the wall meeting the window.

She shivered and turned back to bed, and lay for a long time listening to the thaw, thinking of Sam, asleep now in this very house. Dreaming? There were people who said they never dreamed, but Rosemary didn't see how that could be. What was Sam dreaming of, now, this moment? He must know lots of girls, she thought, and curled into a small defensive position. Maybe one special girl, though he had never mentioned any. A boy like Sam would not be allowed his freedom. Well, she'd met other girls on their own ground before, and won. Abruptly, though she'd forgotten him for years, she thought of Harold Daniels, whom she had taken from . . . it had been from Helena Williams. The recollection brought her startlingly awake. She'd forgotten about that, but Harold Daniels—who had not, as she recalled, taken much winning—had been going with Helena Williams in high school, before he met Rosemary. So that, no doubt, was why Helena had been so cool, so almost insolent, that day with Jay. She has a long memory, Rosemary thought, and pulled her pillow close about her cheek, closing her eyes. She'd met Helena on her ground that time, and won. It hadn't been a particularly interesting victory, but it proved she could do it. With the too familiar pang of self-contempt, she twisted to her other side. Harold Daniels was not Sam Lyons. And, above all, she and the girls at the college did not meet on the same ground. Sam would be leaving here, and those girls would be near to him, involved in the same world. Sorry for herself, angry with herself, achingly aware of Sam here now, but so soon to be gone, she tried to go to sleep. It took a long time.

They discovered in the morning that the telephone men, too, had been about their weary, demanding jobs, and the lines were working. Sam put an early call in to the Deke house and after some initial difficulty ("No, I didn't chop it down, you clown, it fell down. . . . if you'll try to make some sense, we'll have fuel for a comfortable blaze for months, maybe more. . . . I don't know, as many as you can. . . . No, I know a guy who'll be able to get us a truck, so you . . . okay, then, as soon as you can round up . . .") persuaded his hearer to the plan.

Mr. Reed leaned against the doorjamb and listened with frowning disbelief. When the boy had hung up, he pulled at his chin slowly, still incapable of putting credence in what Sam had apparently arranged quite easily. "You mean they're gonna do it?" he demanded.

"Sure thing, Mr. Reed. They're tickled silly, pink, and to death. All we have to do now is get hold of Reg. Where's Rosemary?"

"Kitchen, I suppose. You mean those fellows are gonna come over here and saw the tree for me? No charge or anything?"

"Charge? Heck, no, Mr. Reed. They're—we're—getting a tree out of the deal, aren't we? We have to divvy up and pay for our own firewood, and since we all like fires, it comes to a penny or so each year. This'll last till the end of term, and there'll be some left over for next year. Hope he doesn't get all seniors, come to think of it. We don't want to slave away for next year's generation of hearth sitters."

Mr. Reed rejected the light touch. "It beats all," he said, still in a tone of wonder. "Why would a bunch of college kids want to go to all this trouble for me?"

"Look, Mr. Reed, I wish you'd believe me. The Dekes are coming out on top in this deal. You're doing us a favor."

"That the way you see it?" The man's lower lip thrust out doubtfully, and then he smiled. "Well . . . well, I sure thank you, Sam. You got no idea how much help this is. I was darn near ready to shoot myself, thinking about that tree and how was I gonna—" He broke off as Hank came into the hall. "Sam here's got it all arranged for some young fellows from his frat house to saw up the tree, Hank. Can you beat it?"

"All set, eh?" Hank said to Sam.

"All set. I've been trying to make Mr. Reed understand that it's a good turn he's doing us, but I've just about given up."

The telephone rang and Mr. Reed picked it up. "For you," he said, pushing it toward Sam. There was a pause as Sam listened, and then he began to laugh. "Getting to be a real Tom Sawyer deal. Okay, tell them to come along. But not too many of them. This is our treasure cache, after all." He replaced the phone and turned to grin at Hank and Mr. Reed. "One of the guys from Beta was over there and heard about it, and now they want to get in on the deal. What'd I tell you, sir?" he said to the baffled Mr. Reed, who turned his palms up but did not reply.

Rosemary, in the kitchen with Lenore, had heard Sam's voice when he first came downstairs. Heard it? You don't only hear music, she thought, you feel it. She had felt Sam's voice and involuntarily closed her eyes, thankful that her back was turned to Lenore. They must not, any of them, guess that this had happened to her once again. It's like a disease, she told herself. Like a recurrent disease that you must at all costs conceal. And, yet, the breath-taking pleasure of hearing his voice, of knowing that in a little while, in just a few moments, she would see him again, was more than recompense for the lovesickness she was suffering. She would endure that gladly, just to be near him.

Would he never come?

She turned with a start at his footstep, and his called "Rosemary?" He came into the kitchen quickly. "Hi. Good morning, girls."

Carefully Rosemary laid aside a handful of silverware and lifted her glance to his. "Good morning, Sam." A calm, untroubled voice. Nothing to be guessed from that. "You ready for breakfast?"

"Will be in just a minute. Lenore, I have said good morning."

"Good morning, good morning. Wait a sec and I'll send up this flare I've been saving."

Sam winked at her and turned back to Rosemary. "Could you call Reg before he gets out on the job? About the truck, I mean—"

"Reg is off today."

"Better and better. Well, could you call about the truck? I got in touch with the fellows at the house, just sort of taking it for granted Reg would manage, but I suppose it might be a good idea to nail him down early."

Lenore let out a yelp of pleasure, and Rosemary said, "You mean they really agreed to do this? It seems . . . unbelievable."

"Hardest bunch of people to convince I ever ran into, you Reeds. Yes, they've agreed, and they're of a mind that you are doing them the favor, not the other way around."

"I'll bet," grinned Lenore. "Well, so long as they're willing, I, for one, do not intend to look them in the teeth."

"Look them . . . oh, gift horses. Just see that you remember. Now, how about that breakfast?"

An hour later two cars drew up before the house. A pickup truck stood in the driveway of the Reeds' house, and in the driveway of the adjacent house a large irate man was gesticulating at Sam Lyons and a smallish older man beside him. The boys from the Deke house looked at each other and then back to the trio before them.

". . . told him to get the blasted thing attended to. Been telling him for years. Now look at it—" The big man threw out his arm in an angry gesture. "All over the place, broke my hedge, made a mess of my—"

"Pipe down!" Sam yelled suddenly, and the newly arrived young men looked at him with surprise. Sam Lyons did not ordinarily allow himself bursts of temper. He prided himself on an uncanny emotional and mental balance that overlooked the quarrelsome and the peevish. And here he was, yelling away like the fishwife's husband.

"Sober Sam's got a temper after all," said Bub Holden, with some pleasure. "Listen to that, willya?"

"We've told you the thing was going to be taken care of," Sam was snapping, "and we don't intend to tell you again, see?" He gave a short grunt of greeting to the arrivals. "These guys here are going to saw the thing down and we'll have it out of here today, so unless you want to hold up the works, why don't you beat it and let us work?"

The big man narrowed his eyes. "Okay. But see that it *is* done today." His voice, insolent enough to enrage the calmest person, seemed now to have the opposite effect on Sam. With no further word for the neighbor, he took Mr. Reed's arm and drew him over to meet his fraternity brothers. After a moment's hesitation, the bellicose neighbor headed for his house.

"What was that all about?" said Bullet Anderson.

"Oh, the jerk came out and jumped Mr. Reed before

we even had a chance to explain. Just got my goat, that's all."

"And a mighty entertaining little goat he was, too."

Sam shrugged. "Mr. Reed, these are some of my fellow scholars, and a few stray members from another house. Bullet Anderson, Bub Holden, Myron Brooks, Con Rogers, from the Dekes. And in this corner, Johnston Bailey, Don Rosen, Jay Etting. You got the saws?" he asked Bullet.

"Yeah, Sam. Had to go over to Building and Grounds, but we got three. Have to spell each other, anyway," Bullet said, studying the fallen elm. "Man, that sure was one awfully ambitious tree."

Jay Etting was looking at the house with a curious smile, but before he had a chance to speak, Reg and Hank came out. Introductions and apportioning of labor took up the next few minutes, and then the boys set to work.

"The girls said they'd make us coffee and sandwiches," Reg said, pulling on one side of a crosscut saw. Bub Holden, as the only one present big enough to match Reg, held the other side. The saw traveled back and forth between these two giants as easily as a breadknife going through a loaf of rye.

"Must be some sort of trick to it," said Sam, struggling with Bullet Anderson to release their saw, stuck at an angle further down the trunk.

"If we ever get it out, let's practice on the twigs, huh?" Bullet panted. "I wouldn't mind some of that coffee right now, would you?"

Jay, having little difficulty with Johnston Bailey at the other side of his saw, said lazily, "Get Rosemary to bring it out. I wouldn't mind seeing that little trick again."

Reg halted his smooth motion so suddenly that Bub was thrown off balance. "Hey, what the heck," Bub began, but stopped when he saw Reg's expression and looked around with considerable interest when Reg left his position and walked over to Jay.

"I don't think I like the tone of your voice," Reg said to Jay.

"You don't?" Jay cocked his head and studied the figure before him. "Well, gee whiz . . . fella your size, I guess I better mend my tone. Give me a twenty-word description of the tone that pleases you, and we'll run through it for practice. How's that?"

"You aren't wanted here, Buster. I don't want to have to pulverize you, so take a hint. On your way."

Jay scratched his head. "Pretty sure about the pulverizing part, are you?"

Reg's glance traveled slowly the length of the slim, hard form that was Jay Etting. "Quite sure," he said.

Sam left his saw and came over. "What the heck's going on here?"

"Stay out of it," Reg and Jay said together. No one smiled, though it was, Bullet thought, an essentially funny situation. Movie stuff. And who was this Rosemary?

"Who's Rosemary?" he said in an aside to Bub Holden.

"I don't know."

"Why, sure you do, Bub," Jay said with a slow smile. "Don't you remember the night of the Thanksgiving Dance? The . . . young lady in the orange dress?"

Bub looked undecided, but before he decided what to say, Reg leaned over the tree trunk and pushed Jay to the ground.

"Like I said, I don't want trouble around here, but you get going."

Jay got up, brushing the seat of his pants. "I guess you're right, at that. What do they weigh you on, anyway? A cattle scale?" He turned toward the cars, in the absolute silence of the other boys, and then said, with a laugh, "Presume it's all right with you lads if I take my car? Since it's mine, and all that? Sorry not to escort you home, but you see how it is."

"Go ahead and take it," said Johnston Bailey. "We'll get back somehow."

They watched Jay climb into the car, turn on the ignition, and then lean out of the window. "Could have knocked me down with a hug and a kiss when I found out this was the house. That firewood ought to be plenty hot." He drove off as Reg started forward.

"Relax, Reg," Sam said. "The guy's a pain in the neck and a fool. Always has been."

"Carries things off real pretty, doesn't he?" Reg said in a smoldering voice.

"Yeah. He's known for it," Bullet remarked.

"Gets a lot of practice," Bub said. "One way and another, he's had plenty to carry off."

"Remember the time he pulled Phelps's room all to pieces for April Fool's? Lord, what a wreck he made, and some of Phelps's term paper got lost in the scuffle. . . ." Bullet shook his head in reminiscence.

"And what did Phelps do?" Johnston said. "Why he—"

"Yes, what did Phelps do?" Reg asked grimly.

"Said it was too much trouble, having to go in and mess up Etting's room, so he just took some plaster of Paris and filled the guy's keyhole with it. Stuff hardened like rock and Etting had to sleep in the living room till one of the school janitors came around next day and cleaned the keyhole out."

"But that's the way to deal with him," Bub explained. "Subtle. You got to be subtle. Now, if I was you, I'd lay for him some evening—"

Two or three of the boys guffawed.

"Bub's idea of subtlety is to hit him again before the whistle blows."

Reg looked around at them all, his face relaxing. "Sorry we had this fuss," he said, and grasped his end of the saw. "Let's get back to work."

"The way Sam and I are making out," Bullet said, "we'll be on the same branch next August. Well, let's up and at it."

One by one they returned to the huge tree, and for a while the hoarse progress of the saws was uninterrupted. It was perhaps half an hour later that Rosemary appeared on the porch, slender and appealing in spite of (or perhaps because of, Sam thought briefly) a thick shabby sweater and skirt. She pushed her hair back with one hand as her eyes fell on Bub Holden, and a moment passed before she could smile and call, "Coffee and crumb cake, if anybody's ready." She went quickly back into the house.

Sam released the saw handle from an already blistering hand and said with alacrity, "*I'm* ready."

Only Bub and Reg, at work on the huge base of the tree, continued to saw.

"With you as soon as we get this piece done," Reg said without interrupting the flowing rhythm between him and the quarterback opposite. When the saw had cut through, the two of them stood back, surveying the work so far.

"Oughta get it done today, all right," Bub said, nodding with approval.

"Oh, sure."

If it were done that day, it would be chiefly through their efforts, but physical effort came so easily to both that neither considered it. They blew their cold noses, pulled off their gloves, stamped heavily around to the kitchen door, and entered the babble and warmth in which Lenore was serving as a happy and voluble hostess, Rosemary as a quiet, if not withdrawn, one.

"This is Bub Holden, last of the contingent," Sam said, swallowing coffee hastily to make the introduction.

"Hi, Bub," said Lenore. "You take cream and sugar?"

"All you can get in and still call it coffee."

"Hello," said Rosemary. "It's good of you, all of you, to do this."

Bub's face became a wreathing grin. "Hey, sure," he said. "I remember. You're the girl who danced so good. Nice to see you again."

The remark was made so casually, with such complete sincerity and lack of tact that Rosemary, startled for a moment, relaxed into a smile. Bullet Anderson, who had also been at that dance, had met her with an air of trying to indicate both that they met for the first time and that he had not forgotten meeting her before. It had been painful, and Lenore had provided a quick distraction, in the form of too much talking, almost equally painful. As if, Rosemary had thought, the old unhappiness returning, she were someone attempting to live down a shameful past and being helped in this attempt by loving friends and relations. Bub's cheerful acceptance of her, and his ready compliment, were literally like oil flowing over a wound. She cut him an extra large slice of crumb cake.

They sat eating and talking for another half hour and then the boys struggled into their leather jackets, earmuffs, and heavy gloves, to return to work.

"Now, what do you think of that?" said Lenore, as she and Rosemary gathered together cups and saucers and silver.

"Of what?"

"Don't be dense. There wasn't much college against town in that assemblage, was there?"

Rosemary ran water in the dishpan, stirred soapflakes till they frothed, and began to slide the dishes in. "No," she said at length. "But partly, I suppose, because it's a sort of . . . lark to them. And boys are different, somehow. I think it's girls and the faculty and the faculty wives who insist on all this separation. The girls and wives mostly," she insisted. She felt her sister's eyes on her, but refused to look around and meet them. "Women and girls are always jealous of their positions and scared of losing so much as an inch."

"I'm not," Lenore said firmly.

"Oh, but, darling, you're different. You're like . . . like Beth."

"Beth!" Lenore shrieked. "You mean *Little Women?* You mean that droopy, dreary birds-in-their-little-nests-agree *bore?* Rosemary, you go too far. You—"

Rosemary, leaning both hands on the edge of the sink, laughed as she hadn't laughed in weeks. And it was not, she knew, even as the wonderful humor bubbled through her, entirely the sight of Lenore's deeply indignant face. It was release. It was as though she had finally put something behind and could go on as if it had not existed. It was being in love again, and having a handsome quarterback say she danced so good. It was having Pop's tree, and so his worry, sawed down and carted away by a bunch of friendly boys who might have come from the college or not, for all the difference it made. It was . . . oh, it was uncountable things that made her feel so good, so very, very good.

Therefore it was strange that in the evening, after the truck had been loaded and driven away, uneasiness, emptiness came back upon her like a returning tide. They'd gone out to wave to the departing fleet, and then had stood, she and Hank and Lenore, looking up and down the wet streets. The air remained oddly warm and had spun itself into a light fog that did not actually obscure, but grayed, softened, saddened.

"Doesn't it look empty there?" Lenore said in a low voice, waving to where the tree had stood and then glancing along the depression made where it had lain.

Part of the neighbor's hedge was undoubtedly wrecked. He had come out toward the end of the work and pronounced himself, in a sour tone, partially satisfied, but made it clear that recompense for his hedge would be had. The college boys, to a man, had ignored him, blatantly, rudely, but Reg said curtly that any more talk about it and he would have to go to court. "You be decently patient," he said, "and something will be done about it. Any more of this yapping and you'll have to spend more money getting it out of us than the damn hedge is worth." Bub had slapped his new friend upon the back, but Reg, suddenly appearing far more mature than the boys around him, though he was not much older, ignored that.

There was a litter of twigs and small branches and roots gathered into a pile. Reg had said he'd take care of that later. But above all, there was a bareness in the air, a stark sense of protection stripped away. The tree had always been there, heavy with shading leaves, or strongly, massively bare, but *there*. Part of the house. Part of themselves.

Rosemary, with a little cry, went into the house, and the others followed.

Reg was late getting back, and Sam was not with him.

"He's gonna spend the night at his house," Reg explained, and Rosemary's heart plummeted behind an expressionless façade. "Seems word got around about the tree-sawing caper, and a bunch of people are there to celebrate. A regular burning sacrifice you'd think, to hear them. They're getting beer and sandwiches and lord knows what all. You know something, those guys weren't kidding about being glad to have the tree, work and all. They've got the firewood, and they've built up the stunt till you'd think it was the biggest thing that had happened around there all year." Reg stretched, grinned at her, and looked around. "Where's Hank and Len?"

"Hank had to go home, because he stayed here last night. And . . . Lenore went up already, to study. . . ."

It seemed too great an effort to talk. She sat opposite Reg and stared at the thin flowered carpet, noticing, for no reason, that a corner of it had been turned over sometime during the day and never turned back.

"Something wrong, honey?"

There it is again, Rosemary thought. I ought to be ashamed of myself, I truly ought. At my age, to have that repeated question. She smiled and shook her head. "A bit tired, maybe. All the . . . excitement." There'd be girls there tonight, girls in pretty clothes, the firelight dancing prettily on their faces, Sam watching them, talking to them.

"I guess it's just as well I told them we couldn't get over," Reg said. "I'm beat." He moved his shoulders and arms to ease them, and blinked at her pleasantly.

"You mean . . . they *asked* us?"

"Sure. Bub, Sam . . . all of them. They said since it was gonna be a party how about getting you and Hank and Lennie and coming on back. But, honestly, Rosie, I just couldn't. And Hank said he felt like that tree had been leaning on him all day, so I thought—" He straightened. "Now, look, if you *want*—"

"I don't mind, Reg."

Slow, hot tears trickled down her cheeks. She couldn't help it. She didn't even know why. Because Sam had thought of her, of them? Because she was tired? She didn't know.

Reg got from his chair to her side in an instant, and then she was held in his arms, his hand pressing her cheek against his shoulder, his voice soft in her ear.

"What is it, baby? You tell me. Tell me what it is."

What is it? Almost before she knew she'd begun, she was telling him what she had told no one, not even Lenore, before. She was telling him in stricken, toneless detail the whole story of meeting Jay, and of what that meeting had meant. Her voice, exhuming each moment, grew thin and taut, and her eyes stung, but she went on and on. Endless as the night had been was her telling of it.

". . . and then . . . and then he said, *'You've been practically begging for it all night.'* . . ." She forced each word out, like a bitter pit, and then slumped against him and grew silent.

Reg's arms, firm and loving, remained about her, and he said, "You should have told me before. This is what's

175

been the matter with you, and all you'd have had to do was tell me. Even before I met the guy, I could've told you what sort he was. An unprincipled pinhead."

Even in her misery, Rosemary had time for a start of surprise at that. Unprincipled pinhead. It was not the sort of expression you expected from Reg, and strangely it quieted her a little. She almost smiled.

"Every one of those fellows today think you and Len are swell kids," Reg went on, rocking her slightly, as he would a child. "And not one of them likes the Etting character. Not one. They laugh at him."

"And you . . . you don't believe what he said, Reg? What he . . . thought about me? Because I did dance an awful lot and get sort of . . . sort of excited," she said through an aching throat. "It was . . . the first time I'd ever been—"

"Baby, will you stop? Of course I don't believe him. I know that type. But what's more important, Rosemary —I know you." He said the words with so much dignity and faith that Rosemary let out a long, shuddering breath and leaned against him, almost mindless. "The thing is," Reg said in a quiet voice, "that you're too high-strung. And you've been deprived of things a girl like you wants to have. No college, no pretty clothes. No . . . educated boy friend. So you get carried away."

Rosemary twisted around to look at him. At his old-young face, his gray unguarded eyes, his mouth that rarely uttered original phrases and often mispronounced but was firm and strong and sensitive. This was Reg, as she should have known him, if she'd had the heart and the sense to see. Not brilliant, but intelligent. Not highly educated, but instinctively wise. Not exciting. But something far, far better than exciting. A man who was sturdy, steady, tired from work but endlessly working, filled with patience and a fine good humor toward life. A man who had, through all her nonsense and fickleness and flightiness, continued to love her. Her overnight, all-encompassing infatuation for Sam melted as had Pop's overnight, all-encompassing silver freeze, leaving a bit of fog, a remembrance of wreckage, and a certain understanding that those things would be forgotten in time.

She looked at him in wonder and said, "But why did you wait? How did you know?"

He didn't pretend not to understand. He kissed her, and said, "I figured you'd grow up in time."

They sat together for a long time, not speaking, and then Rosemary said, "You have to go. You have to drive tomorrow, and you've been working all day, and you're tired."

The smile that touched his lips and eyes then was almost like a rebuke, so filled was it with contentment at her concern. But it was not rebuke, Rosemary knew. The rebukes, the reproaches, would all be on her part, directed against herself. Well, she could face that. It was just so miraculous, so much a blessing that she'd realized in time who Reg was. The man she loved. As it was in songs and books and real life . . . the man she loved.

CHAPTER EIGHT

JOHNSTON BAILEY PHONED ROXANNE, WHO PRETENDED not quite to recall him. "Now, which one are you?" she asked, and gave a deliberating, irritating trill of laughter. "The one with the purple weskit? The one who totes a teeny edition of Sophocles in his billfold?"

"Last time we met, I carried a knife in my teeth."

"Yes, yes, now it begins to come back to me. I distinctly recall the teeth. Well, and how *are* you these days? Aged much since I saw you?"

"I've been busy. And it's only been three days. Seemed like years," he added hastily, and Roxanne giggled. "They're having a party over at the Dekes' to celebrate a fallen tree, and—"

"Druids in Newell? I don't think Epke Banta would approve of that."

"You're thinking of dryads. And I don't think the Dekes would approve of that, not much. Now, do you want to shut up a minute?"

"Of course. When is the party?"

"Tonight. Roxanne—"

"Tonight! That's awfully short notice. It's practically tonight now. How will I get my hair arranged? I *hope* you didn't think it was naturally curly. When did the tree fall?"

"Last night. I wish a certain girl I know had been standing underneath it."

"I wish she had, too, if it would make things easier for me. I'm the sort that just can't stand competition. I wilt, I grow silent—"

"You grow silent," he repeated. "Say, did I tell you about the girls I had out last night? Six of them, see, and one brought her sister, so that made seven—"

"Really, Johnny, wasn't that an amazing thing last night?"

"The girls? You don't know the half of it—"

"The ice storm."

"You're trying to change the subject."

"Yes."

"Well, then, yes. It was an amazing ice storm. Don and I tried to get some pictures of it for the yearbook, but there must have been something wrong with the camera." Roxanne, who knew when to be serious, agreed that cameras were often unreliable. "It's really on account of the ice storm that they're giving this party tonight," Johnston went on.

"Roxanne," whispered Anne McGinnis, pulling on Roxanne's arm, "hurry up, will you? Other people might want to make a call, you know."

Roxanne patted Anne's hand in dismissal, continued to listen to Johnston. "Isn't that amazing?" she exclaimed. "And you mean you and all those others went to their house and— Why, it's amazing."

"Don't you know any word beside amazing?" Anne grumbled. "Surprising, astounding, astonishing, singular, unprecedented, awe-inspiring, electrifying—"

"Excuse me, Johnny, there's some mumbling going on here and I couldn't hear you. Go back about twenty sentences, will you?"

"Bewildering, dazzling, monstrous, not-to-be-thought-of, unheard-of, stupefying—"

"All right," Roxanne said to her. "Just a second, Johnny. Okay, brilliant Annie, let me finish up here and you can have it. Five seconds."

Anne said, "Dumbfounding," and grew silent.

"I'll pick you up about eight," Johnston said, "and be sure to wear boots and carry an alpenstock."

"Could I bring Helena along? I'm cheering her up lately. I mean, after all, it's not like a date or anything if it's a house party on the spur of the moment, and maybe you could round up—" She broke off, added, "Is Jay Etting likely to be there?"

"He is not," Johnston laughed. "But that's another story. Sure, bring Helena. There'll be more guys around than girls anyway."

"Then can I bring Anne, too?" Roxanne asked, with a glance at her impatient friend, who lost her look of impatience.

"Sure, sure. Only I think that'll do it, Miss Lonely Hearts. There may not be enough beer to go around."

"I don't drink it," Roxanne said soothingly. "Neither do my sisters here. In fact, we're very inexpensive dates, except that Helena smokes. On the other hand, she always brings—takes—her own, so that involves no expense on the part of—"

"Roxanne, will you hang up?" said two voices together. She turned to find a considerable number of nettled glances bent upon her as she leaned against the wall, toying with the phone wire, finding more and more to say.

"Look, Johnny," she said, straightening abruptly, "I think there's about to be violence done. If you don't find me here, I'll be in the infirmary, visiting hours eight to nine, and I like chocolates, only not the kind with fruit inside—nougats or almonds are fine, and if you could find some macaroons—"

The phone was removed from her hand.

"Johnny," said Martha Greene, "your friend finds herself hauled—I mean called—away. She'll be here, safe and full of sound, I'm sure, when you arrive, and now goodbye." She hung up.

Roxanne looked at them all and smiled. "It was Johnston Bailey," she explained. "We have a date."

"You've already had it, haven't you?" someone muttered.

"It isn't," Roxanne said to Anne, "that I talk so very much *off* the phone. It's just that when I'm on one something seems to happen. I go on and on and on. . . ."

"Somebody take her away!"

Roxanne swept her hair high above her head, turned slowly, and walked down the hall in silence. At her door she glanced over her shoulder and said, "It was at that very moment I'd decided to leave." She disappeared into her room.

Anne, going to dress, continued her catalogue. "Incredible, staggering, preposterous, inconceivable, breath-taking . . ."

When she and Helena and Roxanne were assembled in the living room at a little after eight, she said to Roxanne, "I've thought of sixty ways to say amazing without saying amazing."

"You probably looked in the *Thesaurus*."

"Well, naturally I did," Anne said indignantly. "And besides, they aren't all of them adjectives. And I thought of quite a few just standing there beside you in the hall, remember. It certainly demonstrates that you have recourse to words other than—"

"Where the heck's our date?" Helena interrupted.

Roxanne looked momentarily blank. "Look, dear, he isn't *our* date. Perhaps I didn't make this clear. Johnny has kindly consented to take in tow two of my less fortunate acquaintances, meaning you two. There'll be lots of men, so you fan out and do your best. But the date, the Johnston Bailey, the *doer* of this good, is mine alone."

"Do you know what she's talking about?" Helena asked Anne.

"Nope. The fellow asked the three of us out, so he's our three date. Nothing could be clearer. Trouble with Roxanne is, she has difficulty with terms. She's gotten the plural possessive mixed up with the singular possessive."

"Our three date," Roxanne mused. "Electrifying, mystic, *amazing* term." The doorbell rang. "That'll be Johnny. Shall we lock arms and advance?"

At the Deke house, they had built a great fire, cautiously using only one log from the Reed tree, but ceremoniously laying it on the top. As Sam said, the wood should be dry and excellent for burning, but suppose it didn't burn? "The rite would be ruined," he said.

"I hate a ruined rite," Bullet announced. "Especially when I have blisters on my hands."

"Funny how soft some guys are," Bub Holden said. He looked dolorously toward the dark icy windows. "I hafta go out and get a girl. Sorta wish I hadn't asked her."

"Why, Hercules," said Con Rogers. "You mean a little drop in the temperature disturbs you that much?"

"Doesn't disturb me. Makes me cold." Bub shivered in anticipation, then began to smile. "Say, wasn't that a laugh, that Reg shoving Etting onto the ground that way?"

"If anyone ever asked for a shove, it's that one," said Bullet. "He spreads his implications around like oil slicks."

"Never heard anything too much about Helena Williams," said Bub, settling back as though forgetful of his own girl.

"Oh . . . not the ones he goes with in school here, or he'd never get a nice one. I mean, when he comes back from vacation . . . you'd think he'd walked from spring to autumn over a bridge of compliant women. And the town girls, of course."

"What do you mean by that?" Sam asked.

"*I* don't mean anything," Bullet explained in surprise. "I'm talking about Jay. Far as I'm concerned, those two Reed girls are honeys, and nice kids. But you know how he is, every now and then he takes out a girl from the town—or says he does, anyway—Rosemary's the only one he's ever brought to the college—and then goes about letting it be known that yet another female has succumbed to the irresistible Etting. He hands me a laugh."

"Funny thing, though," Sam mused. "None of us— very few of us—ever do go out with the girls from town. Or bring them to school dances and things. Why's that, do you suppose?"

"You don't get to meet them very much, maybe," Con said vaguely.

"I know why it is," Bub said, getting up and scowling once more at the waiting night. "It's because these girls here in the college they won't let us. I mean, heck, you gotta face it, there's some pretty nice chicks on the campus, and once they get their dear little claws on you, you're sunk. They're a corporation, I tell you, a closed conspiracy. We haven't got a chance. Why, for the luva mud," he exploded, "you haven't even got a chance not to go out with one of the girls right here, let alone not going out with town girls!" He stumped irritably away to dress for a walk across the windy campus and back.

"Did you make any sense out of that last?" Myron asked idly.

"Sure," said Sam. "He has a date and he doesn't want to keep it and he doesn't dare break it. Girls," he ended expressively.

"What're you complaining about?" Con asked, lying on a sofa with his feet on its arm. "You've never gone steady in your life, have you?"

"Nope," said Sam. "I'm just smarter than the rest of you."

"Maybe so, maybe so," said Myron. "But I wouldn't trade Betty for an A in zoology."

"That's a beautiful sentiment. Have you told her?"

"In everything but words."

The phone rang and Con got up and went in the hall to answer it. "That was Bailey," he said, coming back. "He invited one girl and got three and wants to know if it's all right."

"Who are the girls?" Bullet said.

"Roxanne Howells, Anne McGinnis, Helena Williams."

"Tell him sure."

"I did. This party is taking on quite some proportions. You're sure that thing will burn?" he asked generally, regarding the fire they'd laid. "It's a mighty big log the Reeds provided us."

"With all that underneath, it ought to. Boy," said Sam, stretching, "I'd hate to have to saw another one tomorrow. My hands feel like old eagle's feet."

"Tell us the truth, Sam," said Con. "How do you like

it over there? Are you really getting anything out of it for your thesis? All the rest of us are making out fine here, work all day, sleep all night, noses to the note-books—"

"I'm a sociology major, and I've got a special idea for a paper—" Sam broke off, frowning slightly. "Well," he sighed, "I do have a good idea, but one of these days I'll have to explain it to them, I guess. Because from their point of view it might not seem quite so good. Not that anybody reasonably could take offense, but people don't seem to take reasonable offense very often, do they?"

"That's the one thing you've said that I agree with," Con told him. "How about this idea of yours? What is it?"

"Do you really want to know what I have in mind?"

"Sure. That's why I asked."

Myron and Bullet, their attention caught, leaned back to listen as Sam, staring at the ceiling and rubbing his neck, began to speak.

"It's like this. Since I've been in the college, I've been curious about this sort of archaic—or should be—town versus gown attitude, but while I don't really like it and don't think I can do much about changing it, there's no dodging the fact that I've gotten mostly the gown point of view. That is, if I'd come from Newellton, I might have understood the other side a little better, but coming from someplace else, and that not a college town, and not knowing anyone in this one, I was at a disadvantage in trying to understand. Do you see what I mean?" They nodded, and he went on. "Well . . . when we were told to name what our theses would be on, I took town versus gown, and then got the brilliant notion of boarding out in town in as typical a home as I could find. Trying to, you know, get *in* with them as much as I could, so as to get as much out as I could . . . for my paper. A sort of embryo *Middletown* approach. And I suppose you'd say it worked," he continued moodily. "At least, the Reeds did welcome me." He debated whether to mention Rosemary's original reluctance, decided not to, since it appeared from this afternoon's scene that Jay Etting had played some part in her feeling of hostility. He did plan to describe and try to analyze that hostility in the actual paper, however. That would be a matter purely between him and the sociology teacher, something quite different from discussing her here in the house. Sam began to see that research of the sort he was interested in could never in the world be impersonal. He had meant to describe a month in this home he'd called typical—not wealthy and therefore apart from town and college squabble, nor so poor that such considerations would not matter; not a menage of old people, who would have lost or never had interest; not a stupid household—but just what he had found, a lower-middle class, struggling, intelligent family with young people in it. But now that perfect find had been translated into Lenore, Rosemary, Mr. Reed. It had become those particular rooms, where only the kitchen was ever quite warm enough, those daily meals carefully prepared from inexpensive food. It had become those two girls, working and keeping house, that old man, grumpy and boastful and moving in turns. It had became Hank, a kid who should certainly try to go to college, and Reg, as nice a person as you'd meet in or out of a classroom any day. It was not so simple, his plan, as it had seemed to be when he'd had this bright idea a few weeks ago and had sat down smiling at his own cleverness to read the To Let ads. Sentiment was going to try to creep into his writing, and probably a touch of apology, and neither of these belonged in research. He was going to have to be pretty firm with himself.

"Seems a little . . . underhanded, doesn't it?" Bullet asked.

"No," Sam said, more defensively than he'd intended. "No," he went on more calmly. "This is the way all proper research is done. You go to the spot and report what you see, and it's done in an attempt to further understanding. Do you call Margaret Mead's work underhanded? Or Robert Lynd's?"

"No, but they're different."

"They're far more important than I am, and smarter. But you have to start somewhere. You remind me of people who want to be actors but only if they start on Broadway. You have to work up to things, if you really want to get anywhere. You have to start where you can, do the best you can, and go on from there—"

"Down, boy. You're getting overheated. You'll start the fire before the company gets here."

In spite of himself, still a bit exasperated, Sam

grinned and got up. "I'm off to make myself pretty. And the next time any of you guys wants to know about my life's work, you can make up your minds to call around when I'm fifty years old."

"By which time you'll have written *Newellton in Transition*"? Myron asked. His voice was both indulgent and admiring. "At that," he said, trudging up the stairs behind Sam, "I wouldn't be surprised. Not a bit."

"This is an elegant party," Helena said, smiling at Sam and stretching her hands out to the blaze. She wore white knee socks, a green wool pleated skirt, a white wooly turtle-neck sweater. In the firelight her face had an apricot flush and there seemed to be bits of gold in her brown hair. Sam, who had met her now and then, but never with particular notice, found himself surprisingly gratified that she approved of the party.

"Glad you could come," he said. Glad you happened to get seated next to me, he added to himself.

It was, as it had been intended, an informal party. Nobody except the die-hard steadies bothered much to pair off. Roxanne talked at Bullet and Johnston impartially, Anne McGinnis had gathered herself a handsome circle of attendants. Helena, for no particular reason, had wandered over toward the fireplace and found herself sitting on the floor next to Sam Lyons, whom she scarcely knew. All very warm and friendly and tranquil. Helena found it lovely, said so to Sam, and then was startled to find his eyes and hers hold a moment longer than the casual before they looked away. Something fragile and exciting stirred within them, but Helena clasped her knees and continued to stare at the burning logs, and Sam for a long time was silent.

Yes, a lovely party, Helena thought. Suppose she hadn't come? Oh, please do, Roxanne had said. It isn't a date or anything. I just thought it would be fun. Anne is. So Helena had said yes, to please Roxanne, and here she was.

She had noticed Sam Lyons before, of course. With no special, personal interest, but simply because he was the sort of person you did notice. President of the senior class, rumored to be graduating *summa cum laude,* very nice-looking. When freshman registration had been going on—so long ago, only two years and so long—he had directed her to the Bursar's Office. She remembered that, chiefly because in the entire day he'd been one of the few people who hadn't told her the first hundred years were the hardest. But she'd never really talked with him before. I haven't now, she realized with a smile. It felt, sitting here beside him, as though they'd had a long talk, many talks. They had exchanged two sentences. Lovely party. Glad you could come.

The fire stormed about the heavy logs with a roaring turbulent sound, and at its base little flames flicked like cats' paws at the kindling.

"Why do you suppose," she asked, "that they say you can see pictures in fires? Do you see any?"

Sam shook his head. "Just something to say, I suppose. Or, really, to write. Things like that mostly get written. There are some things that cry out to be written, and they are answered."

Helena glanced at him with interest. "Like what?"

"Well . . . like that. Pictures in the fire. Or . . . the stars were so close you could pick them from the sky."

"Pluck," Helena corrected happily. This was the sort of conversation she loved. "How about, she heard a voice crying and after a long while realized it was her own?"

"That's a good one. Don't forget, his eyeglasses grew moist, something seemed to have gotten in his eyes."

" 'It's the smoke,' he said gruffly, and turned his back," Helena giggled.

"Here's a dandy . . . how do you like the moon? I ordered it especially for you."

"And . . . I'm sorry, darling, this is something I'm going to have to work out for myself."

"You've forgotten the portrait that dominated the room by the sheer force of its personality."

"I just hadn't gotten around to it," Sam grinned. "We must have been reading the same books." He studied her face a moment, and went on a little breathlessly, "Are you busy some night next week?"

"Well, gosh . . . Well, which night?" she asked, and their smiles became enmeshed.

"Good," he said. "I'll call you. Maybe every night."

Almost with embarrassment, they looked away from each other. A nervous, rapt embarrassment, too pleasurable to deny or try to overcome.

"Do you remember Sam Lyons?" Roxanne had asked, and, "Oh, sure," Helena had replied, "you'd have to notice him." "Well, he's the one who sort of instigated this fire party. He did something about getting the

191

boys to chop down some old man's tree or something like that. I'm not very clear, really, what he did." "Doesn't sound like anything he'd do, go around chopping down old men's trees," Helena had objected. Roxanne had shrugged. "Just so long as we have a party," she said.

Helena nearly asked about it now, but the moment of vibrant silence was too real, far more important, so she looked at the fire and thought that perhaps there were pictures in it.

Anne McGinnis, bearing Coke and cookies, dropped to the floor on the other side of Sam, and said, "Tell me what this is all about, will you?" She waved her Coke perilously. "Not that I'm not enjoying every crumb of it, the *most* confused stories are ringing in my ears. Did you really steal somebody's tree? Roxanne seems to think so, and Bullet says you went out in a band with lanterns and guns and took it away without a trace. Not even a hole left, he says."

"True as we're sitting here," said Bullet, coming up behind them. "The police will have their work cut out for them to crack this case, eh, chief?" He glanced at Sam and frowned. "Now don't you do the dirty on us, bosso. There's plenty waiting as would like to step into your shoes."

Myron Brooks took a heavy boot and shoved Bullet, not too gently, on the floor. "Did you ever hear of rumors, my friend? Keep this up and we'll be in the Dean's Office trying to explain why we really should be able to get our diplomas like the other people." He looked at Anne and Helena. "It was a perfectly straightforward bargain. We sawed down a tree for a fellow who'd have had to pay to have it done, and in return we got a year's supply of firewood and a lot of good fresh air."

"And a year's supply of blisters," Bullet said, righting himself with a grimace as his palms pressed against the floor.

"Whose tree?" Anne asked curiously.

"Fellow where Sam is boarding."

"Don't you live here?" Helena asked Sam.

"He's on a field trip," Myron said.

"Yes, I do," Sam said to Helena, ignoring Myron. "I'm boarding in the town this month, because . . . for reasons of my own." His eyes said he'd tell *her* later what the reasons were, and Helena took a deep dizzy breath, trying not to make a sound. "But the tree thing," Sam went on, "is simple. It fell down, and you know the rest."

"Was it a very big tree?" Anne asked.

"Yggdrasill," Bullet informed her bitterly.

"What?"

"The tree of life, the great ash whose roots struck through the world. It stood, moreover, in the frozen wastes of the north."

"Gosh, that must have been awful," Anne breathed, and Bullet looked at her with delight.

"Oh, well," he said. "We had a couple of Rhine maidens serving coffee and crumb cake. It was really sort of jolly. . . ." His voice trailed off as he recollected Rosemary's somewhat dubious relationship with Helena.

He'd forgotten, in the pure enjoyment of the Reed household, all about the dance to which Jay Etting had taken Rosemary, and all about the fact that she had come in Helena's stead. That Etting, he told himself, is like the stone tossed in the brook, his ripples go on splashing into somebody forever. He got to his feet, addressed Anne. "In the other room is a bit of what the children call rug-cutting going on. I believe that's what they call it. Wish to join me?" He put out his hands and pulled her up. " 'Bye, all. Unless you'd like to come, too?"

Myron Brooks got up and trailed after them vaguely, but Helena and Sam remained seated.

"That was a sort of sudden departure, wasn't it?" Helena asked. "He behaved like someone who'd almost committed an indiscretion."

"That's a very smart guess," Sam said with a sort of despondent approval. He was thinking much the same things as Bullet had. "I guess I'll tell you something, Helena. I think . . . since maybe we'll be seeing something of each other . . . at least I hope we will?" He waited for her nod. It was accompanied by a shy smile that made him want to reach over and hug her. "Tell you something," he repeated. He did not immediately get on with it, but studied his shoes, trying to find words. "To begin with, I'll have to explain a bit about this paper I'm working on. My thesis. You see, I'm a sociology major, and while I've done a lot of reading and stuff on class distinctions, and racial and social distinctions, I thought that we had here in town a very pointed sort of distinction, a sort you only find in a college town."

"I know," Helena said softly. "I've thought about it quite often."

"You have? You really have? Gosh, you don't know what that means to me." He turned toward her eagerly. "Well, in that case you'll be the one to understand what I had in mind with this paper. Here's a distinct distinction, so to speak, and one right under my nose, so what better theme to take than that? But how the heck can you get both sides of a question if you only live on one side? You can't. Listen, can you wait here a minute while I run up and get a book? I want to read you a quotation, and I'd spoil it if I just tried . . . Wait here. I'll be right back."

He sprang to his feet and made for the stairs. Helena, looking after him, felt a combination of tenderness and respect that she'd never felt for anyone before, except her parents. And that, of course, was not the same thing. As clearly as if they were still before her, she saw his eyes kindle, saw them dwell on her softly, saw them brood and light up and dream. All those expressions, in so little time. And the easy way he'd loped out of the room. The line of his shoulders and arms in the gray wool sweater. Sam Lyons. She drew that deep, silent breath again and waited for him to come back.

"Now listen," he said, settling beside her, a red leather-bound book in his hands. "Listen carefully. This is *Jude the Obscure*. You know it? No? One of his best. Substantially, it's about a stonecutter who dreams greatly, whose mind is profound, but who can't, because of the way he's placed in society, realize his dreams of scholarship or satisfy the hungers of his mind. It's also about a girl whose thoughts are a hundred years ahead of her time, and who is essentially created for a role absolutely unlike that forced upon most women then, and even now, but who succumbs to the ordinary role because that's what her love and the pressure of her times force her to do." Sam's voice had taken on a thoughtful, almost literary quality, not at all like his everyday speech and syntax, and he opened the volume gently to a bookmarked page, reading to himself a moment before he spoke to her again.

"They, Jude and the girl, Sue, are in Christminster, which is a college town, not the greatest, but to Jude it is the Chosen Land, the place of milk and honey, the place where the *scholars* are." He thought a moment. "Well, this is how it goes . . . 'They started in quest of lodging, and at last found something that seemed to promise well, in Mildew Lane—a spot which to Jude was irresistible—though to Sue it was not so fascinating—a narrow lane close to the back of a college, but having no communication with it. The little houses were darkened to gloom by the high collegiate buildings, within which life was as far removed from that of the people in the lane as if it had been on opposite sides of the globe; yet only a thickness of wall divided them.' " He closed the book, keeping his hand about it, and after a moment turned to Helena.

"You see how it fits? When I came across that . . .

that's when I began to think that of course there is a wall, and I'm not going to be able to write a decent, worthwhile paper by merely peering over the wall and trying to imagine what's in the houses on the other side, what the people are doing and thinking. I'll have to go and live there."

"But—" Helena began, and fell silent.

"But what?" he asked intently.

"I was only going to say that while that's a very moving piece of writing, Sam, and maybe there's a *sort* of analogy, it really isn't true of now. Times have changed."

"Not so much, perhaps, as you'd like to think. Oh, the college doesn't tower over the houses and sink them in gloom, not literally or even figuratively, as it did then. But the division is there, the wall is there. You should know. You come from the town, don't you?"

Helena nodded. "Yes, and I know the . . . difference exists. But I don't think it's as bad as you say, and—"

"You should hear Rosemary."

"Rosemary?"

He looked startled. "Oh, for Pete's sake, that's what I started out to tell you. The room I got is in the Reeds' house. And they're very nice people," he added decisively. "Mr. Reed and Lenore, and Rosemary." Helena was silent. "Do you really have a grudge against her, because a jer—because Etting took her to a dance? Do you, really?"

"No." Slowly she shook her head. "No. I had one against her . . . long before that. I guess you'll have to take my word for it, because I won't explain. Rosemary and I . . . just don't get along. But not because she's a town girl—and I'd like to say I hate that expression—and not because Jay took her to the dance. Jay was—" She wanted to say that Jay had been a mental aberration, but you had loyalties, even to people who had none themselves. "Jay was free to do as he wished." In an unspoken pact, they agreed then to dismiss the subject of Jay Etting. "Rosemary's and my . . . dislike . . . goes back a long way. But I really mean this, Sam, I was getting over it before you said a thing about her. I've even thought of her lately, sometimes, wishing maybe I'd been a little more understanding. And not so much of her as of other girls I knew in high school, who didn't go to college. Phyllis Bookman . . . others. But I don't know what happens. Something does. The other girls here don't want you bringing competition around, or something."

"Seems like pretty small potatoes, a reason like that."

"Maybe so. But you do what's expected of you. Most of us do, anyway. I'm not a trail blazer." She looked around the room, back to Sam. "When you were in high school, did they have those secret societies?" Sam nodded. "So did we," she said. "My parents hated them, and the school officials hated them, and I guess plenty of the kids did, too. But we joined them. Those of us who got asked. And we felt sorry for the ones who didn't—most of us felt sorry—but still we . . . avoided those people," she said in a low voice. "You didn't run the risk of damaging your own standing. Maybe because you weren't sure enough of it," she sighed. "It wasn't nice, but it was the way things were."

"I wonder if it will always be this way for people," Sam said. "That some have, and some haven't. Same as this house. I get along great with these fellows. I mean, we all like each other and we have things in common, you know, but I get a queasy feeling, sometimes, when I run across guys who didn't get bid anywhere. Maybe that's one of the reasons we all stick together so much. Maybe because we're ashamed to look them in the eye."

"And maybe that's the real basis for the town against college feeling. We're ashamed, and we're not sure enough of what we have, nor sure enough that we deserve it, to allow any threats to it."

"You're a nice girl, Helena," Sam said. "I'm awfully glad you came."

"So am I." She rose with a young animal grace. "Let's go get something to eat."

"Would you like to dance?"

"I'd love it."

It's always this way, Helena thought, if you get too close to something that's deep, or moving, or too real. You try to get away because you think in a little while it may be too late, you may not be able to get away at all.

She moved lightly, blissfully, in Sam's arms and, even as she thought, forgot about everything but having met him.

CHAPTER NINE

IT WAS THE NIGHT BEFORE SAM WAS TO LEAVE THE REED home. He had about finished his paper, not to his satisfaction, precisely, but to the best of his ability, and there was satisfaction in that. At least, he understood a good deal better how much he did not understand, and that was a step toward learning. He'd come here rather cockily assured that a month among the natives would provide him with all the information a student sociologist could wish, and he left the better for a dawning of humility. The better, too, for the gaining of two acquaintances who might one day be friends.

That Hank and Lenore were so much younger than he seemed to matter not at all. They met him on a basis that had no reference to age, nor, for that matter, to town society. All along he had divided Newellton in the two factions, deploring it at times, forgetting it at times, studying and analyzing it much of the time, but fundamentally sure of the cleavage. And it was surely there. What had not occurred to him was that there would be people to whom it meant nothing at all. Lenore was sorry not to go to college, for no reason

200

except that she wished to study, and Hank met everyone as a person and judged him so.

"But, look here," he said now to Hank, as the two of them sat talking, "suppose you do go to college, what makes you sure the same thing won't happen to you? That you won't just drift away from the people you know and go around with now, if they don't go to college but go out and get jobs?"

"I think sometimes all of you people who talk about this thing miss the point," Hank said. "One of the points. And that's that people's interests change, and their needs change, and the fellow you batted around with in high school may be just as unconcerned with you as you are with him, after you both get out of school. It's the school itself keeps a lot of people together. Take that away, and it shows up that you just don't have much in common. Whether you go to college or not doesn't alter that. Any friends I have now, real friends, I mean, I'd have later on, no matter how we organized our lives." Hank looked thoughtfully at Sam. "But most so-called school friends are really school acquaintances. Fun to be with, and then you drift apart because that's normal. It happens to people all the time."

"You don't think there's an—animus between the college and the town people here in Newellton?"

"I think there's a difference of aims, and I don't think there's much effort at understanding, on either side. And there's snobbery and jealousy. On both sides. That sort of thing would always be stronger in a college town because the differences are so defined. And I don't like it, but, lord, Sam, I don't like so much that's going on in the world."

"You can't just say that and do nothing."

"Didn't say I wasn't going to do anything," Hank smiled. "I intend to work hard, at college if possible, but at something else if that doesn't pan out. And try to keep my wits about me so that I don't get sucked in by high-sounding phonies. And try to be . . . a good neighbor. All small stuff, personal, I suppose. Not the proselytizing view. But I believe in small advances. Each man doing his little best," he ended, a bit self-consciously, but firmly.

It would be to everyone's advantage, Sam thought, for Hank to go to college. What a fine teacher he'd make. But whatever Hank did, his essential value as a person would not change. Given enough people like that, each doing his small best, as Hank put it, and the world might yet crawl out of the pit into which it had tumbled.

"Have you thought any more about yourself?" he asked. "About going to college in the fall?"

"Heck, Len and I haven't thought of anything else. We could swing it, I think. It would mean putting off getting married. Lennie wanted to get married and work while I went to school, but I don't know . . . it seems to me a marriage ought to start out on a different basis than that. I guess she agrees, really, because she gave in. Oh well—" He sat up with an air of finality. "It'll work, perhaps. We'll see. What are those girls doing in the kitchen? Firing a new set of china? If they'd let us help, the job would've been done hours ago."

"Before we go in to see, would you mind if I incorporated some of your ideas in my thesis?" Sam asked, and then snapped his jaw shut as he realized what he'd said. He'd meant, some day, to tell them about it, but not just yet, and not tonight.

"My ideas?" Hank asked curiously. "How would my ideas fit in your thesis?"

Sam sighed and began slowly to explain.

". . . so, you see," he wound up, "that it might very well sound the way Bullet put it, underhand work, but I honestly started out with the intention of trying to analyze and understand a situation that certainly exists, one that bothers me, and ought to bother anyone who takes the trouble to think about it."

"And how has the paper worked out? What did you put in it?"

"The house itself, as much of the background of the family as I could get from talking to Mr. Reed and the girls. Mainly it concerns Rosemary and Mr. Reed, because Lenore doesn't seem to be much affected by the town-college thing. Rosemary is so rabid about it that perhaps she isn't typical. And Mr. Reed . . . he doesn't like the college, there's no doubt about that."

"No, there isn't."

"You think I've done something underhanded, too, is that it?" Odd to wait so tensely for the opinion of a boy five years younger than yourself, Sam thought, and waited.

"No," Hank mused. "No, not by your lights. Or even by mine. You set out to write a scientific paper and went at it in the most sensible way you could manage.

I think you might have mentioned it, but I suppose you thought they'd alter their ways, or something."

"Exactly."

"The thing is," Hank told him, "that while I see what you're getting at, and Lenore probably would, too, I'd hate to have Rosemary know about it. Rosemary . . . is a strange girl. Very proud, and bitter. She's felt this thing more than anyone I know, and she's gotten worse the past few months. Tell you the truth, I was surprised that she was ever even civil to you, much less as nice as she's turned out to be."

"Maybe Reg had something to do with it. He got along so well with the fellows from the house, and she's in love with him."

"And that's another thing," Hank muttered, but when Sam looked inquiring he refused to amplify. "Just thinking out loud," he said. "Sure, use what you want from all of us, Sam. That's the way progress occurs, isn't it? Scientific building on observations of people? But, for Pete's sake, keep it from Rosemary. And from Mr. Reed, too."

"They're perfectly private themes, you know. Only the professor reads them."

Hank got to his feet. "I'm going in and drag them out of there." He lifted his head and sniffed. "Well, what do you know. Fudge. Smell it? They've made fudge."

Reg came in later, with his invariable pizza, and they all sat together in the kitchen.

"A farewell party for Sam," Rosemary said tranquilly, nibbling at the fudge.

"Oh well, now," Sam protested. "Not farewell, really. I'll be around."

"Of course you will," Lenore said. "And we'll miss you, too."

Rosemary did not second that. Not, Sam realized, glancing at her, through any dislike of him—he was quite sure her dislike had vanished, though unsure just why—but simply because she was looking at Reg and didn't hear the remark. Yes, a proud and bitter girl, and Sam didn't think the marks of hurt and longing would leave her soon. Perhaps never. But she was happy in her love, a love obviously far deeper and more meaningful than it had been when he came here only a month ago, and it was possible that love would soothe, would some day erase the bitterness, if not the pride.

"Well, I'll miss you, too," he said, looking at Lenore.

He would, for a fact. Glad to go back to the house, to his own room, shared with Myron and Bullet, but sorry still to leave here. Only a month. It seemed shorter. It seemed longer. Peculiar how months could go by that you simply didn't notice one way or another and then one would come along—sometimes even one day would come along—and everything would be changed. One day he had known Helena only as a girl who used to go around with Jay Etting. Now he knew Helena, herself. Perhaps she'd tell him sometime how she'd happened to get mixed up with Etting, and perhaps not. It didn't matter. What mattered was that now they knew

each other, and their thoughts had a disturbing, a wonderful way of mingling. They had met as though resum-
ing a friendship interrupted but never lost, and Sam,
who had taken many girls out and once or twice felt
his heart begin to move away from him, knew that he'd
never met anyone like Helena before. That combination
of prettiness and no nonsense, of sober interest in words
and works and sudden frivolity. No other girl like
Helena. . . .

The other night he'd had dinner at her parents' house.
A house very different from this one in which he sat
now, chewing on pizza. A house placid and spacious
and glowing. And yet he could imagine, though he
didn't see it, people eating in that kitchen, too. There
were certain people that Sam thought of as four-dimen-
sional, people who would be at home anywhere. His
own mother had the quality, though his father did not.
Hank had it. Lenore, almost. All three Williamses did.
Mr. and Mrs. Williams were the sort of adults who were
interested in what you had to say, but never so interested
that you knew it was politeness or condescension to a
youth.

"I hear you share Helena's sporadic guilt complex
about the division of troops here in Newellton," Mr.
Williams had said, as they sat down to dinner.

"Troops?" said Mrs. Williams. "What a way to put it."

"Warfare, in its way," replied her husband. "Armed
truce, you might call it."

"And it isn't sporadic," Helena defended herself. "I
never really forget it. I mean, something in me remem-

bers, just the way something in me remembers that it's cruel to set traps for animals. But you can't go on thinking about things all the time. You know they're there, and now and then you hope you can do something about them, or you try, but gosh, there are so *many* things to think about—good things, too, and you can't even think about the good ones all the time."

"And a fine thing, too," said her father. "I never would have wanted to be one of those Upanishads, meditating in one direction all my life."

"I don't think you could *be* a Upanishad," Helena said doubtfully. "I think you study them."

"Either way," said her father, unperturbed. "The point is, as you said, there is too much in life to waste it in one way of thinking. And, of course, most people couldn't, even if they wanted to, the mind being what it is—tricky. That's what accounts for the great turnover in volunteer social workers, I imagine. All honest compassion—and it is honest, I'm sure—and then, poof, you've got a chance to go to Florida, or your nerves are shot, or something similar, and the call goes out for another volunteer. Very human."

"Very cynical," said Helena.

"Not at all," said Sam. "It's just about what you were saying, only it's concrete. You worry from time to time that girls you know are being hurt, but you don't do much beyond the worrying, because you can't. Short of organizing a union or sending a petition around, I don't see how any of us can change the setup in a town like this."

"The methods you suggest," said Mr. Williams, "would mummify the system. As we are now, flexible enough, with kids like you thinking the matter over among yourselves, going into the town to find out about it, there's a chance that in time things might actually alter. Not much of a one, I grant you, because there's nothing society hugs to its collective bosom like inhumanity. What would we have to aim toward and write about, without inhumanity? For that matter, what would we have to go to war about? No, no, inhumanity can be tempered, but I doubt if we'll ever bring ourselves to do away with it entirely."

Sam looked at him uncertainly. Was he serious, cynical, or just having fun talking? Something of each, perhaps.

"Well, there was one point made in that little sermon," Mrs. Williams said to Sam and Helena, "which is that if something's to be done, it'll be done by young people having an interest. It's too bad that you lose your ardor for progress as you get older, but unfortunately most of us do."

"Well, there's one thing *you* don't do," Helena said to her mother, with a sideways glance at her father, "and that is quit your volunteer work at the Baby Clinic. Daddy carries his role of skeptic too far sometimes."

Mrs. Williams bit her lip, looked at her husband, who gazed back with no expression but the merest flicker at the corners of his mouth, and said with a slight sigh, "But darling . . . your father and I were thinking of going to Florida."

. . . Sam threw back his head and laughed.

"What's the joke?" Reg asked, and for the swiftest moment, Sam blinked, so completely had he gone back to that other evening, leaving this one.

"Oh . . . something I heard the other day. Too complicated to explain." He looked around at them all affectionately. "This is an elegant party."

He meant it, but, more than that, he enjoyed using the first words Helena had used to him. Words, now that he thought of it, he'd never have heard if it hadn't been for the Reeds, for the storm, for his having thought of this idea in the first place. But Hank was right, probably. He'd never be able to explain his paper to Rosemary. He'd heard that Rosemary was called boy crazy, and though he'd seen no sign of it himself, he thought perhaps that was because of her feeling for Reg, which seemed to deepen—heighten—grow in all ways recently. Being boy crazy, or girl crazy, it seemed to Sam, was probably just a seeking for the ideal, the perfect love, a seeking that becomes frantic through never getting what it needs, or perhaps not even knowing quite what it needs. Well, Rosemary had apparently come to the end of that search when she realized what Reg meant to her, but what she was doing instead was to retreat into a world that contained only her and Reg. She as good as denied the college existed. Take that day, for instance, that they'd all gone ice skating—a bunch of people from the college, and Hank and Lenore. Rosemary had been asked, but she turned the invitation down with barely an excuse. It was clear that she was now prepared to ignore the college as much as the college had ever ignored her. The difference being, Sam thought with a rush of tenderness, that the college won't know. She was such a nice, prickly, proud girl, and he hoped very much that in time she'd learn to live with life instead of constantly holding it off, suspecting it of treachery, trying to pay it back. Reg would help her. But it would be better, wouldn't it, if she tried to help herself? Sam, one of those rare people who spent more time thinking about those around him than about himself, considered Rosemary thoughtfully until he found Reg's equally thoughtful eyes upon him. Then he smiled and said, "Sorry I was staring. I got to thinking about something."

Lenore rose. "Sam must be tired. He's so absent-minded. I *am* tired, so goodbye, Hank, and goodbye, Reg, we'll see you tomorrow."

The following morning after breakfast, Lenore said it was a pity that Sam would have to leave with no one to wave a hanky at his departing back.

"But work and schooling must go on," she said, struggling into her boots and straightening to smile at him. She put out her hand. " 'Bye, Sam. We'll see you," she said, and was gone.

Mr. Reed had already left, with a perfunctory handshake, almost as if he'd forgotten just who Sam was. Mr. Reed always parted from his lodgers in this manner, recognizing that the relationship was over and no benefit to be received on either side from a pretense of affection. Sometimes he neglected to say goodbye at all, as with the gym teacher, whom he had thoroughly disliked. He did mutter, as he left, that it had been darned nice about the tree, but even that was briskly said. Sam and the boys had done an excellent job of convincing him that the transaction was entirely to their benefit. And so he walked down the street, jamming his hat on his head, and put Sam out of his mind without a notion that the advent of Sam had changed all their lives, including his.

Rosemary was the last to leave, and her goodbye, unlike her father's, sounded warm, and, unlike Lenore's, sounded final. She had liked him. For a day and a night she had thought she loved him. She was quite prepared not to see him ever again.

"You know," she told him as she tied a scarf about her head, adjusted her coat, and turned to face him, "you sort of remind me of *Pippa Passes*. Everywhere you go, things change, people change. And you just go along, being your unchanged self."

Oh, but I'm not unchanged, Sam thought. I'm very much changed. He did not say this to Rosemary. "As I remember, most of the changes Pippa wrought were fairly good ones. There's that."

"Yes," Rosemary said pensively. "Yes, there's that." For the first time she lifted her eyes and fixed them full on his. "I hope, Sam, that your paper will be a success. That you got all you needed from us."

Sam, taken aback for the moment, felt his face redden and then smart, as though he'd been slapped.

"Well," he said, after a painful silence, "I guess you . . . Did Hank tell you?"

"I read some of it. It wasn't very nice of me, but then— I was cleaning your room one day, and you'd left the thing face up, almost as if you were intending for someone to read it."

"No," Sam said. "No, I didn't intend that at all." He wanted to add something but could not think of one word.

"You think I'm angry, don't you?" she asked. He nodded. "Well, I was, for a bit. I was . . . hurt. When I read—" her voice assumed an air of quotation "—'a never adequately warmed, worn-out house, homely and threadbare' . . . no, wait, let me finish. You'll see I know it by heart . . . 'like a very old animal waiting for the end. But when they are here, the two girls, so different but both so alive, and even Mr. Reed with his unpredictable moods, the old animal lifts its head, smooths its fur, and decides to live again.'" She stared meditatively over his shoulder, and he did not dare break into her thoughts. After a while, she resumed. "When I read that, I was furious at first. I called you a sneak and a spy and a betrayer."

"Called me? To whom?"

"Lennie."

"You mean you both knew about it?"

"Yes. We talked it over. And it's a funny thing, Sam . . . we changed my mind about you. I mean, we decided that you were honestly trying to understand and analyze something that Len and I have felt the stings of for years. And we decided you were very smart to do it this way . . . going out in the town, living with an actual town family." Was there a barb in her words, or not? Sam couldn't decide.

"Did you read any more of it, after that?" he asked. What she had quoted was the opening paragraph.

Rosemary looked at him scornfully. "I said it was almost accidental, my reading that much. I read that, and no more. We don't make a practice here of going over people's papers."

"I don't suppose," he said hesitantly, "that you'd care to read the rest of it, the whole thing?"

"I don't believe so." She pulled on her gloves, picked up her purse. "No, I guess not, Sam. Thank you for the offer, but, you see, I'm past caring how this age-old problem gets itself solved, or even if it does. It simply doesn't mean anything to me any more."

"I don't believe you," he said impulsively.

"No?" She put out her hand. "Still, that's the way I say it is. Goodbye, Sam."

"Goodbye, Rosemary."

And now the house was quite silent and empty.

He climbed the stairs to finish his packing, and tried to think what the next boarder would be like. It must be grim, this having to take strangers, one stranger after another, into your home. But then a lot of things were grim. Injustice, poverty, cruelty whether or not it was deliberate. It's all there, he told himself, impatiently, part of our world, and we can't just say we never made it, so it's no concern of ours, the way Rosemary is trying to do. Life might appear at times as if it were without kindness, without reason, without justice, but it occurred to Sam, in a puzzled, hesitant, but not to be ignored moment of vision, that life might have to be treated as you would treat a difficult relative from whom you could not part. Looked at one way, there were so many things wrong you couldn't begin to count them. Suppose you stopped trying to count them and took the relative as he was? Probably what was good would have a chance to come through, and perhaps what was wrong would be amenable to some change. Whether it was life or relatives, you never seemed to get anywhere while your fists were clenched and your tongue was sharp as a sword. It was incredible, but still for that moment in the empty house, all of life presented itself to Sam as a stern, waspish, unreliable aunt, standing with her arms at her sides, her face defiantly lifted, a bigoted word on her tongue, and as he watched, a word, a gesture, softened the stance, quieted the word, gentled the eyes, and you discovered that there was mercy and gallantry hovering beneath the rigid surface. With effort, with understanding . . .

Sam moved his shoulders suddenly, and glanced around the room, as though someone might have caught him in such a strange vision.

"My aunt, Life," he murmured to himself. "Let me introduce you to Life, my aunt."

Then he grinned and snapped his suitcase shut and started on his way back across town, to the college.

Set in Linotype Caledonia
Format by John Rynerson
Manufactured by The Haddon Craftsmen, Inc.
HARPER & ROW, PUBLISHERS, INCORPORATED